THE
TERRIFYING
ANGEL

ALANA EISENBARTH

THE
TERRIFYING
ANGEL

an exploration of madness from the inside out

THE TERRIFYING ANGEL

Light Realm Books
Copyright © 2014 Alana Eisenbarth
Cover image "Domestic Stranger (edit)" by Chryssalis

Printed in the United States of America.

ISBN: 0991464907
ISBN-13: 978-0-9914649-0-6

for the Suicide at the box office window

The mind acts like an enemy for those who don't control it.

The Bhagavad Gita

PREFACE.

Whatever it is in us that creates division in the human beast had taken up residence and was again eating its tail, slipping into the poles, reaching and attaining another darkness or plunging farther into flight. Whatever it was that had punished and scolded itself, had cracked and reached for the blade to render itself free, its intention not death but killing as the Steppenwolf kills the day, as an angel might destroy a life in its presence simply by magnifying beauty beyond a sustainable form.

Therefore, there would have been an angel wrought of bronze in the cathedral, and one might have prostrated herself in its apprehension, in apprehending metal scored and banged into a hollow form whose eyes not being formed but out of negative space—what is carved and left out, what is vacant and seeking and unfilled—became defined by a black panel of wall.

How an epiphanic instance might define a plight; how one might see, mirrored in the metal hole, herself; how one might sense or know what she contained and be in awe of its capacity to destroy, to devastate, crush level annihilate completely the beautiful, to extinguish, so that it too became a thing of terrific beauty, so that what she apprehended in the metal form was life and in that living form a merciless creature hung.

What concerns this story is inner world, so that its exploration would be at the center. Entrance would be an emotional charge, a feeling that took us deep. We, and by we, I mean the collective, the multiple self that we are, would begin to explore what had struck at our surface from the moment we recognized the self in our surrounding, from the moment we saw our reflection in the world and that reflection contained such fierce beauty we wanted to know it.

Imagine every memory has become a place within you, a room of the psyche where parts of you reside. Imagine you could follow a feeling so deep inside that it took you inside of us all. So it is I have come to understand the self and what lives within. What follows is a lyric journey into that underworld. It is a dark descent, and long. I mean to emerge with a heroine at the end, an archetypal figure to lead us on. For that to happen, however, we must see ourselves as we are, recognize the world of our making, that darkness has a role.

As it does not interest the mind, what happens as a sequence of events also does not interest this story. It is racked from a brain forced conscious. And so I shoot a thousand arrows throughout the book's unfolding, letting them fall to the ground at the end and land where they will, like the seeds the ancestor scatters, knowing that each will land in its rightful place in its most auspicious rendering of truth in a realm that is and is not ours, one that is seen and unseen, experienced as wholly as the human vessel allows.

PART 1.

THE EMPTY VESSEL. It is the boy again with the tenderized hand, that red thing turned out from the body like the child we can't seem to love. And we know we're in danger when a vision comes to mind in such violence we scarce believe it, until that vision quickens and becomes many, until we find the emotional crux of this thing, until we are met with the smell of our own blood on the cutting board, the heat of escape sickening the fear with love as a loved one ties us off and pushes us into the back seat of the car, our sleeve flooding with blood. I am ashamed now to be heading where I am, ashamed to be returning an empty vessel.

VICTIM.

I am waiting in the chapel for the woman to wash my clothes, which are soiled with blood from the cutting. It is late, and the rest of the ward is asleep. If yearning could draw things from nothing, I wonder, what would save me from this? My spine is a wooden knob pressing into the pew; I am a Dali clock grounding itself on a concrete floor.

I feel the darkness of his hollow eyes and the merciless thing they belie before turning to face the angel from the cathedral. The corner of his mouth is brazed as if with a pale stain of blood. Singed metal radiates from his shoulders into wings, a great sword crosses his chest, and a shield, grazing his cheekbone, ends at mid-calf, its coldness expanding into the space like the absence of breath, so that as he falls to the floor, it could be birth, each fall, and death.

"What is this?" I ask, suddenly aware of the shame in my mouth at his closeness; black thread woven through my forearm.

"It is victim," says the angel, his voice trawled and raw. Slowly he lifts his tonsured head, his green eyes shockingly bright against his wan skin. What is left of the bronze cage cuffs his neck like the talons of a great bird that has discriminately released him into a chapel filled with light. Strength gone from his arms, he takes hold of the pew in an attempt to rise, his naked form still posed on falling, one leg tucked beneath the other outstretched, so beautifully animal in his nacreous skin. It is just this paradox that draws me; that he is both bird and prey echoes what I've been seeking to understand within.

"What are you?" I whisper.

"If I asked you the same, how would you answer?" He retracts his wings, faltering slightly. "Things are not absolute. You see extremities that do not exist but in instruction. They teach us wisdom in this way."

"Do you mean the visions aren't real?"

"What is real, Aurora?"

What is real is that someone has finally come. Whatever he is, I am not alone, so that the fear that sweeps momentarily through travels on. There is nothing to capture it, nothing to hold it to my chest like a harrowing wind that erases all.

FORGIVENESS.

The inner realm has grown hostile. It is why the angel's come. How do I explain what I've known from the beginning, that half of me wants me destroyed?

The room that I enter is dark, the light source undefined until at the back a woman stirs. As she steps forward so moves the light, her face long in it, her body formless, that I see not so much the pear or coil, but its offering of luminosity in darkness.

"It took me by surprise," I begin. "I reached out in sympathy expecting it to be reciprocated. Instead, the twisted thing set a trap; the game began and I was pawn. He could feign emotion, could use it, but could not feel. Something in him had gone terribly wrong, and I took pity stupidly thinking love might save him. But who am I for savior?"

"You blame yourself for this?" the white witch asks. "What right have you?"

A child enters the room, a girl with blond curls and sprite blue eyes. She wears a royal blue dress with yellow cornflower clusters and a white pinafore trimmed in eyelet lace. The woman rises and plucks a lollipop from a glass apothecary jar marked 'Cyanide' on the back edge of a desk. I watch from the settee as she hands it to the girl who shakes it from its cellophane and twirls it into her mouth all the while surveying me with a child's curiosity. When she has sealed her lips over the rainbow-colored disc, she slips her chill fingers into my hand and begins circling the settee in game, humming and passing her arm over my head as I lower myself in allowance. Unused to children, I watch amused as the little blue dress goes around and around, and the child giggles and stops. She drops to the floor, her skin pink like gum.

"What have you done?" I cry, falling beside her body, which ticks as if charmed on the pea green carpet, her tiny hands waving at her throat, her rolling head thumping the base of a bookcase lining the wall. Thump, a cat at the cupboard eager for food. Thump, thump. I set out a fevered hand.

"You've just watched me poison her," the white witch responds, this wise woman, crone, assembling from beauty a form. (Yet wouldn't her features have to be crooked and her look severe to warrant such a mien?)

"She's just a girl!" I intone as the body writhes and leaks out a cry.

"You could have stopped me." Her voice has not strayed from its pedagogic tone.

I tug at an arm, steady the head, somehow responsible, somehow akin to the wickedness of the crone. The body stills, its sapphire eyes coming to rest on a corner of the ceiling as I search for some life in her neck until the woman snaps, "Leave her. She's dead." The acerbic tone pinches the heart and allows a flood of dark felt in. I don't want to be here.

"You trusted me. Why?" she proceeds.

I lift the girl, stagger to my feet, and weave toward the door. "Please. She needs help."

Her tone is louder now. "You trusted me because you had no reason not to, and because you assumed I would not hurt a child."

"What is your point?" I am still walking, waiting for the woman to tell me this has all been a farce, that the girl in my arms whose weight is 1000 pounds is not dead.

"Forgive yourself," she demands.

"And she'll live?"

"Forgive yourself."

"I don't know how."

"Look, had this sadist a sign you still wouldn't have believed, just as you overlooked my 'Cyanide'. We can't go through life holding others suspect."

A sigh from the corner draws my eye. There a boy balances on a stack of boxes, his head over a folded knee, his arms shielding his face.

"Do you know why he's crying?" the crone asks as the boy's eyes meet mine; something has been pounded out of them.

I shake my head. Is it sadness?

"And yet you feel compassion for me?" It is a voice I know. I feel my cheeks go hot with fright and the words *I bet you'd let me fuck you too* soughed into my ear, tripping me, so that I'm crushing the girl to my chest as I fall. I have nothing left for this, and the girl is a doll, a warm ragdoll, absorbing my tears as I slink down to floor, unable to go any farther.

The boy has quills, and I am bleeding.

"What is this place?"

"It's consciousness."

"Some are too broken," the crone says, finally, before taking my good arm and leading me back to the bed. The boy is no longer visible.

"So I should stop feeling?"

"Never. You are perfectly sensitive. This is a gift. Connect with it. Never use it to hurt yourself."

WITH A SAVIOR I COULD.

With a savior I could walk through this room unafraid. But he? It would be dark for him, and he would know the wind for how it felt rushing through broken things, dashing itself quickly lest it be afraid. And so headstrong and obdurate the angel falls, into trees, into a forest where what had contained things in heavy glass jars has dented the lids with its beak. Birds, each sounding its note more beauteously that it be caged.

You would have to know darkness to be here. You would have to proceed through the vacuous dark. For here, I am a shade on a branch, a shadow trapped in a former self. What frees these things when the impetus to do so harms? When the tyrant has walked away, hands in her shirt sleeves, water in her throat, for it has rained and she too is contained here within? And what of the one who keeps singing?

You, battered thing of warbled hue, mashing your beak into paste and smearing the walls. Do not stop singing, you. For somehow you'll keep me alive in all this, a pitch careening into glass but not shattered. Here, we are not metal but glass.

"What is that song he keeps singing?"

"It is his own," the crone answers, "for to ask the self not to sing might murder his heart. What you hear is dying, drawn out. What you hear is sound throttling itself, for in darkness what is tortured gropes the walls, its talons drawn, its flesh picked and picked and picked off in a dying night that flashes at times in storm. For what darkness could possibly know itself without light?"

And so picking might draw flint from the night and we might know in a flash what was caged peering out, faces in fire, then night drawing in again at the seams of the cage. Then the angel will surface cursing himself, cursing and flapping his disheveled wings, snapped shafts swinging belligerently in the draft that rises as he tries to rise...

KIN.

"How did you know about me?"

"In your trauma you revealed the light realm; I merely followed."

"There was no light."

"Then you saw its shadow." I am astounded by the profundity of what he reveals and his casualness in conveyance. "Something in you sought its existence. It's all around you."

The angel is naked and bruised. We are kin.

He wants to explain how light is beyond comprehension of judgment; it merely fills spaces where love is depleted. Aurora's body is shaken, however, and the gravity of the wounds she's sustained settles in, so that she weeps now in inconsolable self-pity. He watches her chest heave beneath the thin hospital smock, auburn hair falling past her shoulders, cropped pieces forming a crown, the drawstring pants and pale naked feet, her gray eyes lit and cheeks flushed in temper. It is such that what had anchored him within her now ousts, and he's lifted into the warmth thrown from the candles as it negotiates the draft coming from the windows lining the south hall. Heaviness overtakes his limbs, and he sets out a hand to steady himself as a woman enters and the door clicks closed.

Discontent inspires change in us. It is only growth.

THE ANGEL AND THE WAR THAT BEGAN THE WAR WITHIN.

Cold mist wakes Nor in mid-fall, and his wings unfurl with the opening of his eyes—lashes and feathers soft and wet, black wings on a black night. An empty arbor of steel bars demarks his progression, swift the patterns changing overhead. He is a gift to the world, a healer who has not quite shaken martyrdom. The beauty of this landscape astounds him, so that he stretches his feet out before him and drifts down as with parachute over the black lake and night-drenched trees, illuminated by a thin crack of light arcing out of the sky. The water is still but for facets of moonlight reflecting a pulse beneath the surface.

From beyond the ridge of trees comes the sound of cattle plodding the hill, their hurried hooves drumming the ground as his feet seep into the cool, soft grass, and earth slips between his toes. He can hear the cattle now in the woods trampling what's fallen there, a hoof ground into a rock ledge as a cow slips. A shade moves into the branches above, a bird of some sort, and he knows what has to be done as on foot, he follows the creature through the copse. At the end a man waits, his brawny form dwarfed by Nor's in approach. The man sniffs at the angel and scratches a thick patch of beard. Dark hair covers him and forms a mane to his shoulders. He wears a ragged cape of brown felt under which a piece of fabric falls to mid-thigh. His feet are bound in leather to the calf.

Nor speaks a form of Gaelic. Go easy, he says, and the man

leads him to the lake's edge where water laps at the bodies of four cows lain out along the rock beach. As Nor moves towards the cows, the man sniffs him again at which the angel lowers his head. Aurora. *Had I touched her?* He smiles and pats the man's back and then crouches beside the nearest body and lays a hand on the cow's side. Life returns in the form of warmth. The animals are merely stunned Nor realizes as he touches one after the other, and within minutes, they rise dazed and amble off in the direction of the herd. But this is not why he's come.

There is a group of men sitting on the floor of a cave. God has promised to come and bomb the city. Nor hears their dialogue in a foreign tongue. A woman sits with them in the garb of a man, her face, uncovered and sweetly masculine, her form slight. He has understood that she is in danger. When something speaks through her, she is a bird, throat torn, screaming out across the desert with Nor in flight overhead. Her cry speaks of apocalypse. It speaks of dark crime after dark crime. It curls from her lips in black smoke and pours heavily into the cave until it solidifies and is belched from her lungs like wet charcoal. What follows as the men sit and watch her dress fill with black is silence. Then the instrument of body is tossed aside, where it crawls toward the entrance unseen.

"Remember the dark thing. You will need it," Nor says, interrupting his story.

When he finds the woman, she is on a ledge overlooking a city of white stone. The city is doomed: her skin condemns it, her arms and back scored with a light that radiates from her core. The light burns out, leaving on her skin symbols burnt black, a blister of frost covering her in a powdery surface like the scales on a moth. She loses consciousness and falls. Although Nor can smell the burn, the woman must rise. She must be taken into the city. He does not know how or why, only that they must go. People are flooding from their homes. The one they call the Prophet has been told by the angel Gabriel that a woman will come, that they must heed her warning. She and Nor must go. This has all been prophesized.

"Why?" Aurora wants to know when Nor tells her this story. "Why doesn't Gabriel tell them himself? Why must a woman be harmed?" But who can answer such questions? It is why we come into this world.

"Some of us live as symbol," he says with downcast eyes.

They enter the streets where the woman gains consciousness at the crowd's touch and stiffens against him in pain. She wills unconsciousness to return, that god of grief, that she might leave her body to be read like braille. Wipe it clean of its charge, she wills the people, a hand plunged into her side, and the angel transports her deeper into the congregation, invisible to all but the man who had received Gabriel's message all those years ago. An old prophet now, he nods at Nor and looks toward a sky old with heaven, his long, white beard tied into the waist of his dress.

The next day the city is decimated, brought to ruins by the cave-dwellers commanded by God, but the people of the city, having followed the Prophet into the desert will be saved. Having known God's protective hand, the city-dwellers will live to return. In fervor, they will begin reconstruction. In the months that pass, they will work hard, their faith spurring them on, enhancing their efforts with perseverance and strength. The Holy Spirit, they will say.

Yet the cave-dwellers will lay siege again, this time without warning. The same who have salved the girl's burns will seek her out. They will find her in the temple wound-white and weeping while the city falls to bombs. They will drag her into the streets, where she will be trampled in stampede. Here, Nor will find her, and on her body the unclothed words. When he lifts the woman, he scuffs them out of the body he drags.

The woman is nothing.

"Oh, Aurora." Nor watches her hands flit to the heart. "How can we recognize what doesn't recognize itself?"

Fire and black smoke pour from the ruins where a dying weapon chatters in a far wall. The angel wades through the rubble; the powdery sky falls in a hush. How everything feels dead here: the city he'd help defend, the woman in his arms that he drags. How from the distance something comes closer. He feels it as shadow in the periphery as the soldiers crawl from their shelters, file out in lines, pour out in hoards, hedging piles of rubble, his voice drawing them like metal filings so that they fall at his hands like dolls, tiny colored dolls which he dismisses as all armies are dismissed.

Like this, he has tired of sweetness. Had that war another end, had he not been there as witness. He wants to be immune, a machine of God if he must, but immune to such suffering. His arms are filled with a cloying scent that he cannot rid himself of as he slams into the floor of the hospital. He is filthy from the war, filthy from falling from trees, filthy from the darkness of his thought, the soil shielding his nakedness.

In time he will have words for it, a cerebral counterpart to explain to himself what is happening, to explain to himself what he feels. For the moment, it has to do with sacrifice, with cutting and tying oneself to a bed. It has to do with a girl and a religion and denying the self so that one might cast off all she is for another. How the other could be anything.

A CRY. A BURNING. *If you can imagine for a moment what was forged in flame forever carrying that flame, containing it, sustaining it like a cry held out over time, all that has ever and will ever hit that pitch becoming one and holding it out. Eternally. Metal angel. Glass jar. All that is born in flame. That a woman burning might burn for what she contained. That all of these things might be one.*

DISCONTENT.

The angel is there when I wake, his wings filling out over the space of his back, so that I feel their presence expand into the room and then retract in respiration, like blinds being sucked in and out of a screened window. Inhale. Crinkling parchment muted with cloth. Exhale. Static unfolding, feathers sweeping a tile floor.

"Whatever we give credence to reigns," he shares in disgust. I realized that the day the towers fell; some were feeding a virulent god. "I could serve that god, too," he says. We all could. The disheveled brown and bronze wings collapse. The inner landscape's been trampled. I try to rise, but deflate.

"I can't," I say from beneath the blanket.

"Then stay in bed a while," he says despondently, his mood reflecting mine, and the thought, *stay*, lightens something with its permission.

Then the boy in the office spits. Hatred returns with the sound of breath and accordion wings. In my hand there's a blade, which shuttles toward the heart and stabs. I feel the thud as fist clops against breast, a deluge pushing at the hand. I will fall forward on emptying. That is all. Through the blanket the angel takes my hand; something tremors through then dies.

"You see things," he says. It is a question that knows its answer. Is he in my head? I flip the blanket down to find myself staring at the pale green stones of his eyes. He is crouched on the floor before me, wings like a mangled rucksack curiously towering over his bare torso. "What do you

17

think they are?"

"God trying to contact me," I say, leaning forward for confirmation, so close that sand filters down from his wings, but the stone reveals indifference. "Well, that was at first," I amend, retreating back down into bed. "I've since read that they're hypnagogic or hypnopompic hallucinations and not all that rare."

"Does that make them less spiritual?"

"Only when I think of them as glitches in the mental process, which are essentially what hallucinations are." There is sand in my eyelashes. When I lift the hand that's held his to my face, it smells of burning and what makes me hunger, displaced, to be found.

"Maybe God speaks in glitches," he says.

In the mirror at the far side of the room, my cheeks appear to hold the heat of fire. Damp hair falls in dark strands across my face. There's a smudge of black across my left cheekbone marking me. I wash my hands with a tiny bar of hospital soap then hold them to my face again. What is real seems to be what we perceive as reality and what influence that perception has on our character and mind. Anything we believe to hold truth is real.

"So reality is subjective." Nor responds to my thoughts.

"I know only that I seem to perceive a world that many others can't; that I am in constant communion with a spiritual realm. Sometimes that language is energy, the way we know something is wrong before it happens, the way we sense the presence of something before it arrives." I am conscious of my body crossing the room. "Some of us are more susceptible to these energies, and we use them to understand the world around us and live more deeply. When one doesn't however sense them, then they are not part of her reality and appear not to exist." I pause a moment and reach for the cardigan draped over the back of a chair, then add, "You are the first tangible manifestation of what I've believed to exist."

Pulling the sweater over my shoulders, I resume my spot on the bed. His tattoo appears metallic the way it carves into his neck like a brace, stirring what in me longs for escape.

"Nor," and as I say this, I struggle. "I imagined a psychic, a medicine woman or healer. I never thought how this might feel coming from…" I look at him reclining on my bed as if on the ceiling of a Roman cathedral, only his form is not rotund, the flesh not overwhelming, not obscenely round but more Blakeian for suffering, the way wings can be powerfully frail, the arm joint smashed, the way a god might wield its power from the ground. What am I trying to say? That I am dying in his presence that I'm nothing more than a wounded thing. The member that lies on his leg is nothing I incite or arouse. I'm crestfallen, clenching my arm to my chest, hurting myself physically the way he is hurting me, the pain pacifying enough to go on. "I imagined she could see something surrounding me, an aura perhaps, something that marked me, something only she'd been trained to see. She'd have some insight for me, a message or, I don't know something enigmatic, something that only I would know the answer to. Then I would know; it would be clear. I would not wonder anymore why I'd been created. I would no longer want to destroy…"

"And I imagined God," he says, taking me in his arms.

I close my eyes. It isn't until sometime later when a siren soars out over the night and something crashes into the hallway at my door that the silence is broken and I open them again. The light then coming through the windows is cold, the sky overcast and gray. It makes the furnishings in their metal and wood frames spare and sad.

"If an idea makes you feel bad, reject it. If it makes you see the world as banal and trite, it isn't true. Beauty is truth, truth beauty. This is God's world (and Keats' I attribute), and God (Keats) wants you to feel good." He smiles at me coyly.

"Then they're God-sent."

"It makes you feel good to think so, right?" I prop a pillow against the metal headboard and nod. "Somewhere within it fits; it resonates here as truth," he says with a hand on my chest. *Nor, I can't breathe.* "God is always in contact, Aurora.

Through the interconnectedness of all things, the divine has its hands always within you."

Nervously, I run my fingers through the back of my hair, working through the tangled mass. Snarls have formed at the base of my neck, which I'm ripping as I separate.

"Are the visions meant to affirm something then?" Broken ends scatter down the front of the blue and white johnie. "Are they oracular, symbolic?"

"I don't know. Maybe all those things. Were you fearful when you saw them?"

"God no, in awe of their majesty. It was as if something had hinged itself on the cusp of our world. That I was witness to the light realm. That something had opened me to it, allowed me passage." I stop touching my hair. "But on the other hand," I continue. "These things come when the mind is in trauma, when I'm troubled or depressed. I've woken to see the rafters draped in golden webs, thick cords of light spanning the ceiling, a spider the size of myself overhead. What they offered was a glimpse at what I can only describe as divine. A divine presence, something asserting itself as strongly as my will was giving out. I needed it to be divine. It had to be. You see, as if it were sickness."

"Your world troubles itself excessively with classification. Pathology. Embrace the mystery."

"I do." I sense that he knows it.

"We find ourselves the longer we live," he begins in explanation. "It is a process and meant to be a process. If I'm an angel what does that mean? That I've a greater connection to God, that I do his or her work, that it's assigned, that somehow the assignment is known, that I'm somehow more aware of things?" I'm nodding my head. Yes. "The truth is, I am more like you than you imagine and these conveyances from God are as enigmatic as the ones you receive. It is only that our perceptions differ. God compels me from within."

I am reticent. There is something in me that draws from him. *Don't speak for a moment*, I will him. If we expect God to come to us from the outside, but it actually comes from within… "Nor, we are vessels. When we fail to pay attention on the inside, the message is transferred outside of us as something we can see. Could this be? Essentially, that hallucination is God reaching us externally from within?"

Bravo, Aurora. We can't discount any of this.

THE VEHICLE OF A GOD.

Had the angel remembered certain things it would have been easier. For instance, that Aurora could not have known that he had been there all along although he sensed that she sensed it; and that they could not communicate but through symbol, and that those symbols might be enigmatic and vague and might cause her to want to suffocate herself or drown or wrap the body in rash. In this way, she will be in danger.

Nor won't recall this, however, until it is too late: the vehicle of a god in communication with itself, an angel, a shape-shifting thing now conscious. How the Other moves like an apparition, a silent film, a deer, a flock of bluebirds, a snake or vine, neither one thing nor the other, but everything in corresponding need. Suddenly, like the return of a theme in the concerto's second movement, he has a past.

A ROSE HEWN OF PAIN.

So the nightingale pressed closer against the thorn, and the
thorn touched her heart, and a fierce pang of pain shot through
her. Bitter, bitter was the pain, and wilder and wilder grew her
song, for she sang of the Love that is perfected by Death, of the
Love that dies not in the tomb.

From ***The Nightingale and the Rose***
OSCAR WILDE

So it begins with a girl cast to the wayside, a rose hewn of pain,
a nightingale torn, what does not know it is frozen to the floor
of a house within. By within, I mean where we dwell in
question, where the wise woman waits as guide, where dark-
ness is a bird, is a daemon, a god. Therefore, the within house
might resemble a house I'd known, wooden and remote,
stripped bare in the body/mind. I would call it the House of
Winter, for winter was perpetual there, the girl on the floor
perpetually frozen.

What resides there is something I've destroyed, something
I've tried to protect by killing it temporarily, something of
myself that objected to what I'd become, so that it wouldn't be
safe to wake her until I had cleared off the damage I'd done.

What we temper seethes. You can't contain this; it writhes
and reorganizes. We are not asked to be but what we are.

Tell the story of the one within who would destroy.
How many times?
Till it breaks you. You will be other.
But I can't now.
There is a rift between you and the angel.
Angel. Winged beast. Beauty.
Yet you reach for him as if he were all goodness. Who said
an angel was goodness? Maybe he's transport, vehicle, a way
down inside. What would he know of the dark but its traverse?
And then he would love you.
Love and an angel. A man dying on a cross. What do you
want? I can't anymore. That goddamned bird!
Yes. Angel as bird, a thorn through its heart, a rose.
I had become the bled thing.
But we pick up from here, having chosen the patriarchy.
Anything bleeding, losing life in fluid, that squid that you'd
hung, the bird, earth. Enter the dark. Ask for something. Or
continue to compile what are they symbols, conceit, what are
they?
Artifice.
We have no need for these things, for what is real is within
you. You are the story of human finding itself in God. God not
wanting to be found.
No, God not wanting to reign. God as observer changing
everything, the microcosm of the cosmos, what is in itself
expanding.

CAPTIVITY.

How animal restraint and how it fuels animal and animal rises, wants to belt, to ravage and scream as the patient is thrown to the ground before me, his hands twisted up his back. Before I can make sense of the scene, the doctor who's been summoned, a pert, officious woman, hair in a sleek taupe knot, releases the needle from his neck and glances at her watch. She scribbles a quick note on the clipboard she's been handed and glides from the room, the patient, strapped to a gurney, wheeled off behind.

"Faelan, schizophrenic," says the boy who plops himself beside me on the floor, the introduction thieved and abridged from the numerous 12-step meetings we've been forced to attend.

The space is gray-white and expansive, the walls blank and empty, industrial, clean. A circle of red plastic chairs forms its center.

Aurora. Bipolar, borderline. I don't like this game.

Faelen tucks his knees into his chest then relaxes them and begins to sketch on the pad he's lain over his thighs. From time to time, a creature appears on his block illustrative of a disorder. A patient peers through a thickly pelted limb, or downed wing. Electra is a startling portrayal of a winged beast with the face of a girl parting the pinioned wings and expansive breast, a girl with wide set eyes and skin like scales. The face is duplicated, the eyes at various stages of closing, so that as one

25

peruses the page the girl blinks to life. The next is a crowding of birds and beasts with mouths stretched open wide. Their eyes are Nor's. I gasp when Faelen lifts the sheet and with it the arms of the sky, and there is release in the vortex of light.

"It's the light realm you spoke of," Faelen explains although I already know. I also know I shared nothing of the angel in group.

"What do you think happened?" I ask, uncomfortably casting a glance across the room. I am referring to the boy they'd wheeled off, recalling his hands twisted on his back and crushed. I've been trying to understand how violence forces its way inside, how in the face of the restrainer I'd recognized a punisher, that smirk leaked across his chin, brightening high on the cheeks as something within rejoices at causing pain. What is this deviant thing that escapes through the visage as you cut?

"Some don't want a closer look," Faelen answers.

"And you?"

"Some of us see everything regardless."

"They're amazing," I say, touching the page and sensing something undisclosed.

"Eh, they're just sketches." Faelen hurls the pad to the ground.

"You don't really believe that."

"No? No, you're right," he says, leaning awkwardly over me and scooping it up again. On his knees, he fumbles for the pencil, which has traveled a greater distance. He slips it behind one of his ears, which being large and elastic, causes it to spring forth and drop onto the floor again. This time, I pick it up. When I hand it back, it is to a trembling hand.

"Meds," Faelen says in explanation, shoving the pencil into his khaki trousers then taking it just as swiftly out again as he settles back down. I meet his blue eyes. His hair is sun-brown, shiny and cropped close to his head. His hands are flat and red like meat from the brick they're thrown against. I will write a poem about him. Faelen will fall in love.

"You could look like that," I say, motioning clandestinely toward the cubist-looking form crossing the room, his pasty white lips giving him a monstrous look of allusiveness, as if he moved through his own caves. "He-uh," I make a dumb monster noise meant to put him at ease.

"Or that," Faelen says, catching on with a laugh so quickly retracted it hiccups out and jerks at the hand pointing across the room to a nurse who looks like he's been fattened with formaldehyde. The nurse's skin, yellow and thick, leaks from a blue pullover at the center of the jar, his eyes drifting in their swollen lids until they come to rest on Faelen and me, who shrink down, caught.

Faelen flips then wildly through his pad, and I spin and scoot toward him as he comes at last to Self-Portrait, a wolf in a storm of paper drawings. The wolf's parched lips open on a bubbled "Yowl," and a string of drool hangs languidly down. In contrast to Faelen's other drawings, this sketch is comic and self-aware, and there is judgment in it. How he manages this, I can't quite grasp. I scratch an itch at the middle of my back and then hand the pad back. My look is pensive as I face him again.

There are some who can see within us the flight we take from self, some who see the bird set in the face, a scarlet fright with pinioned cheeks, some who can flatten and sever and reveal the one within we would have destroyed. And so he takes me in like one watches a crime, probing my features while his hand moves adroitly over the pad. Just as I have learned in pitch blackness to write in straight lines across the page, so has he learned his canvas, never looking down. Slowly, as a figure emerges, it dawns on me, what I couldn't grasp: the existentialist bent in his portrait; how he will sever my world from divine. I feel a lethargic tug at my core—that strange black spine of the stranger. *Oh Faelan, tread carefully by*. Instead of asserting myself, however, instead of telling him to stop that I don't want to see, that it's too much for me to know how I might appear to him stripped from my guise, I swallow thickly and lay my body theatrically across the floor.

Drama is allowed within these walls; it is what makes them so comfortable. One has the freedom to react to anything emotionally, a freedom forbidden in the world.

"Not your thing?" he provokes, turning his drawing into critique, but whether he is hostile or it's my own skewed perception I don't know. The beige carpet smells like stone. It is rough against my cheek as I lie there in surrender, and Faelan nudges my ankle with a red-footed sock. (Is his sock red? Does it matter? Inside it feels red.)

He nudges with his stark realism until I am spinning circles within a wall of blades, a woeful girl, a simpleton knight. The harder I stare at the fantastical rendering, the more acutely its truth stares back. It is as if his perception stripped things to the level of their fears, as if what he portrayed defined me: Aurora, the deluded dreamer, slipping the world into her mouth, the naïve child covered in shame. Everything he's drawing I've tried to destroy. Stupid, stupid girl. I fly at him, eking a deep line across the sheet. I claw at the pencil in his hand.

I want them to come then, the nurses in white coats. I want them to cover the world that he sees, the way that he sees me, the way that I'm not. I want them to stop him, to stop me, to stop.

THE BROKEN. *We are looking for something to control us, for the outside to entrap us, to punish, to cage. We have not yet learned the emotional range of the human animal. That is why we're here. We've been conditioned to rely on systemic restraints: institutions, jails, schools. They will wrestle the demon back into the cage, sedate us or admonish us and free us again into the world. But we will have learned nothing of what we are or the powers that we house. We will have accepted our fate as deviant strains. We will have welcomed our diagnoses and with them the license to be deranged. Our minds are faulty and diseased. We are the broken ones. We cannot help what we are.*

WHAT I'VE ASKED FOR.

"Bullshit," exclaims a man in doctor's garb with a tonsured head. *Nor?* I'm racing through the corridors, trying to escape. I cannot in flight, see his face, cannot tell until I stop, and until his eyes betray him and his pince-nez, and I fall forlorn against the glass: this man's not Nor.

Someone is sliding a metal door. Someone is tossing me a cape. Something surfaces and begins to draw a shape from the chaos, a woman's form, incomplete and complicit.

"Let's get out of here," she says, leading me.

The yard is fenced, barbed wire ringing the top of a 20-foot concrete wall that sits about 200 feet from the path. Not having been allowed out for some nights now, I'm touched by a giddiness fed by the cold. I look around at the few trees dotting the courtyard and tilt my head reverently toward the stars. I neither speak nor feel the urge to arrest the stillness as we wander toward the chapel where a shallow spire looms.

"Do you know what I see in you?" the white witch questions beneath the eaves as a mist begins to fall.

"I think I do."

"Then you also know just as you've asked for me, I've sent for you."

I have felt the truth of this without it having come to cognition. I nod and face my mentor when without warning a shower of debris falls from the spire.

BLACKBIRD. HOUSE OF WINTER.

We were being watched, and what flew down from the spire was not what I'd imagined at first, dander or plume from some bird, but glass, in one shard and then many, splintering to the ground like a storm that changes everything, so I am sent to my knees like an animal that knows only its predators have increased, and that it stands no chance; the heart like a black sack deflates. Whether one believes or not, one empties the furnace of self; a dark blast of air seeps into the basement pores, the crevasses into which a finger swathes the cool powder; residue coats the hand. And the glass—had there been a window, but there was none—fallen from the sky, so that what takes me and drags me through is ruthless. It derides me, sniffs my hair and spits it out, sweeps my feet from beneath me, reflects a visage, flat and plain.

What could love this defiled thing?

"I don't want to be here."

"You must," answers the crone.

For we are on a plain in an internal landscape, and there is the ebony god flitting about at the margins of self, a dark-winged thing in the distance raising its wings in challenge, foraging the sky for its *Opfer*, its victim. Its burnished skin stretches over a metal frame, thick plates tick by one another and the warrior climbs the sun-singed clouds to their height. When it gnashes its wings over its broad back, fire breaks out. Perpetual burning. Perpetual war. One side holds the other in balance.

"Walk here, Aurora, and even the warrior draws his blade

against you. It happened within before ever on the outside," says the crone.

"Show me again," I tell her.

"The ones at the window. The ones with their faces always at the glass. Match the darkness within the room with the night's. Pitch black draw the switch. There a man looking in. What he wants you can gather from the scream that shudders you awake before the next quelled consciousness. You've asked to know these things."

But I haven't. How could I have?

I see my body dragged, fabric trailing the ground, pale feet that could be dead in the mud, for they flail out as the creature hastens, drag as she slows, she, lugging ugliness until I am haggard with it and the body becomes a death-white corset, slung low over her shoulders and clamped to the waist like a breastplate of lead. She is scraping my toes on the ridges, crawling around through mud and dark rain. When she finally stops—the old stone saturated, cape torn from the glass, soiled and tangling my pale legs—I am the light that flashes from her limbs in the darkness as the ebony figure turns and draws to the side like wings or the curtain of some forbidden stage, the dark cloak, yet I am beyond all these things.

"Do you see that?" the crone asks.

"Yes. Shhhh."

There is a child in the house, for the chapel has become a house, its gray form molded to the frozen planks of the floor.

"Aurora," Nor's voice soughs from the ground. *The angel has muddled everything.*

Where is he? I'm crawling, sidling up the house, trying for some reprieve under the eaves when laughter shudders from the trees, and the murder in the bleachers shifts to get a better view. A gray mass of clouds distends, something snitches a strand of hair from my head, and the angel takes a half-hearted swat which misses. Hands held to heart, I stagger away, Nor trailing closely behind, when the thumb-plugged cry of a blackbird draws our eyes toward the sky. Is it this that pulls a dark hole into my chest? Is this the tyrant by whom I've been dragged? But there is no reprieve with the inner world stung as it is and this bird picking flesh off the heart with its shards and dark wings.

There will be no tenderness here. You will be alone in the cage. To touch would ask me to destroy you.

Who speaks this?

There is a feather scraping the lining of the chest, a nail scratching at the lid.

Again the grit of the wooden stair as I feel my way in darkness into the stagnant air of the attic where the moon pools from the low window. I want this to be beautiful, but it's not. What has happened to the body has been no mistake. Coyotes rasp here. Lady bugs sheared from trees come again to die within the pantry walls, within the attic, their movement breath across my lungs, nap of wings writhing against strings, rising within me as a voice I can no more control than swallow.

"Where are you?" asks the crone.
"In a house I once knew."
"Tell the story."

I am alone. Without, there is nothing; without, the silos in winter. Beauty drowned in the season's pool. Snow so frigid its arms are wrought black. Will you know where I am? What I'm telling? Memory is that place in the body that lives as we wander, relives, quantifying details in parts: a house, a coffer, a bird, a girl white and bewildered falling open on the page, when all she could tell me was *Safety. Rescind.* So that what he takes from me in vast, beautifully white sadness, is not a bird though I feel within the flit of tiny wings.

So that I don't know which I am here, the self dividing out so wickedly. What is soft within has been tossed off into a clapboard room caked in snow and ice. Face down the girl lies in the perpetuity of winter, where snow forever falls, where it fell on her body, the pale skin, the thin gown, until it became coffer, until she receded, until I felt only the absence of warmth within, a stiff doll I could not wake.

Here you will see how I treated loneliness, how I let the body be gone from me, the vessel in cataract. Here you will blame me for what I've done knowingly, for she did not fight, could not, for the victim knows only to stand down, hands thrust upon itself.

So the bird shuts her dead in a bell jar.

Faces ascend into windowpanes; darkness smudges the

house. I will see it in daylight and know that they've come, that they've been here in the night, that they'll be here again. They were coming inside with their darkness, so that it would always belong to them; what they'd reached on the inside would always be theirs.

I see my breath drifting out across floorboards strewn with sand; the house frozen beneath my cheek, my slate hands, the tops of my thighs cold-nailed through the joint. A dead leaden arm lifted and dropped. Blue-gray contusion: the sky puddles out overhead.

I don't know which I am here: girl or bird.

A REALM ON THE CUSP.

The girl whimpers from the floor, and I am again outside. I see her through the stones as the angel rounds, as trodden and sad, he fetches his wings and casts them against the house.

"You knew what you'd done." (It's the angel.)

"I'd swept her off into the house. Don't come down here with me." There are things we tell no one.

It's too late, however. Nor has already descended. The scales he will leave on the house, a dusting like moth wings on the stone that he rounds, as he sidles against it in fright, for it is dark here and what does an angel know of darkness like this? The blackbird has learned the house and the world beyond. How I have taught her darkness and cold, how I have taken what she was and swept it clean, saying, this is real: this house; this is real: a specter and an American game; this: love, that says wait, how can I?

The silos in winter. This is what I am. Empty gray metal and wind. I curl up, leaving that space open on my chest. I don't want to touch its rawness to my arms.

"Goddammit, Ror!" he says, turning against the walls. "You drew stories. It was why an angel would prostrate himself on the concrete floor of cage, before you'd tempered the girl with fright, before you'd had the cages blown. You lived in a realm at the cusp of the real one, a realm in which everything had influence, in which heat ticking through the walls at night became a metronome metering the moon across the sky. You could brush your hand against the

36

needle and slow the pace of night. It would become a leitmotiv to the taking down of your heroine; metal and hollow and what would expand. You made us believe this. Remember?"

I don't remember anything. There is only sludge in my chest, something holding me down.

"Why would a warrior take a sword to herself?" the crone asks from the corner of the courtyard where she has remained since the glass fell through the sky.

"To spare the world a fake." I do not look up from the ground.

"Is that what you are?" she asks.

"I don't know what I am."

"Can I tell you what I just saw?"

"I'd rather you didn't."

"You can go then. Get some rest."

I am surprised to find the offer genuine. How she observes me then, as if the skin on my forehead were transparent and beneath its paleness images passed: black wings flitting beneath derma.

"Come now," she says, coming from behind and tugging me from the armpits.

Yet my body is distended and getting it from the courtyard an impossible feat. Heavy darkness pushes through like cold knowledge, like grief, like shame we lie with alone because it is ours, this mystery, because it bores into us like another time has made it welcome and rides us bare-back from within. It matches vibration with shame, and I sit on the floor for grounding.

"How often will you come here, Aurora, before you see the senselessness? Before you come to realize you've been tricked again?"

THE ABJECT ONES.

When I return to my room, light comes from a crack in the bathroom door. Something ticks against the washbasin. Slowly, I breach the doorway to see the angel's gashed hands drawing over his lathered head, a blade stroked punctiliously from back to front. Basin and floor are littered with curls. A scarlet laceration stretches and thins to his waist, where a white hospital towel is draped high, and his wings hang from his back like the stand of some doll. Despite the seeming violence, his countenance is bright. Has he done this? I stagger deeper into the room when a hand greets my cheek with the smell of rust. I lean into it until it's taken away then watch as the white cap is reduced to a strip above his right ear and shaved clean, the blade rinsed and dropped into the sink.

"I have been sent to heal the abject ones," he says quoting one of my notebooks as he takes my hands to his neck and wraps them over the bronze collar. It is my own neck, my own broken thing, and the warmth of it recalls the image of a bird on a rail. It is something I won't remember until now: severed, the bone piercing through skin, a yellow cord coated with sand. The tide moves in the light, darkens and brightens and darkens again. The vortex of sky, the vortex of skull, I hold the head. Is this something I've done or will do? The heaviness falls.

"I can't protect you," he says. "It is not what you ask of me. We are here to live, some hard. Our experiences expand us. Our capacity for felicity and pain, love and hate grow us."

"Do you know of the bodhisattvas?" I ask, dropping my hands to my sides. It is on the same page as the line he has quoted. How can he protect me?

"Those who devote themselves to suffering that they might heal the world," he responds flatly while bracing himself against the wall to dry his wings.

I hedge the sink.

"In my writing, that piece you quote, I will have discovered a place inside of me of all suffering, a dark expanse. What I have felt it to be I will have read to me in a passage on bodhicitta by a Buddhist nun. There is wisdom in the traverse of darkness. Why I sit in darkness until a consumptive pain hollows memory into a well of abject need, I will better understand. That these meditations make me human, I will not question. That there is healing at their source, I will believe. Whether it is an expression of love for what is human or merely a need to surrender to the beauty that inhabits the entire range of human emotion, it is within me." I pause. "But sometimes I hate human, Nor. Sometimes I want to kill it for its sensitivity."

"I know," he says, drawing a hand over his scalp, drawing his head down, pinions widening then drawing in over the space of his back.

"It seems so paradox in the world that sensitivity is hailed as weak. It is not weakness though, and sometimes I find myself striking out at the self for not fitting the grain."

"That is why you can't fight him." He looks at me with revelatory brightness as if the woman before him had changed form.

"I see what he carries and it is like what atrophies there contains me."

"What did he have, Aurora?"

He must be within me or how could he know? I do not answer for some time. "What draws sickness in me, what says in me that my knowledge makes me part of what he's done, and so we become what takes, together. I can't deny it is the self, and I don't want to live anymore."

40

He reaches for me then, awkwardly and self-consciously, fingering the bandages, climbing my arms. When he stops his hands are like braces, mechanical and hard. My worth drops before him, briars stuck in my mouth, dry, brittle scabs of stories, things I wanted to say. I feel his repulsion for the thing he's forced to console, and I stand there, forcing myself to take it, to hold still against him and let him take what he wants. What shone is dead. What lit me is fallen.

Let me go.

The woman turns against the mouth's wall and swims away. What was follows her into the dark throat.

Nor wants to tilt her face back up, so that he can gauge what she's thinking and never hurt her again. There is reverence in her, what values the individual, the idiosyncratic nature of other so much that it will not assert itself for fear of destroying the beauty of those around it. Something has crushed her, laid her out and taken. She will not be this thing.

PATHOLOGY.

Sleep has been tormented by the berating one within. I wring the sponge out over the sink and watch as gray silt runs over steel then gurgles in the throat of the drain. Outside the earth smells of wet stone, mildewed panes, and still water. It hangs its melancholy in dark, vaporous clouds throughout the grounds of the institution. A shade passes over the window of the art studio, and I look out to see nothing but a few trees being wildly slung about by the wind.

I slide my hands into the wet pail below the worn oak table and sink my fingers down into the clay, removing a softball-sized chunk. The plastic taped to my skin shifts in the water. I retract my arms and turn my wrists to examine them as the water drains from my hands back into the pail. What had the crone seen in me? My thoughts shift, cowardice stalking me, as I shuffle back to the table and stand before the mound of clay. A face emerges slowly as I work it, imprinted with thin veins from the bandages, which sit low on my wrists crinkling and disturbing movement. Frustrated, I crush the clay back to nothingness and slip my hands into the cool mass again before smoothing the surface with water. What is this thing inside of ruin? Perhaps the clay will answer, I think, and try again. I choose no form, however, simply move in the way the inner world tugs, so that my movements are heavy and slow and without intention.

I'm no good at this. A dank draft sweeps around my ankles, pushing past pant legs and thoughts. A ponchoed man steps into the room and stomps the rain from his Timberlands. With a large, flat hand he pushes the hood from his head and searches the room for the instructor, who is standing on a table hanging a colorful mobile of tie-dyed tees from the fluorescent lights. The man tips his umbrella into a corner, and my eyes dart to the clock. Seven minutes to nine. I throw a dampened towel over the mound and cast another glance at the staff sent to fetch me. He smiles. I half-smile. He stamps off a bit more rain—rain, which has seeped beneath the cap and clings in white drops to his nappy head as he hangs it in the doorway, watching and counting the seconds that he waits. Fifteen, sixteen, seventeen drops on the parquet floor.

The art instructor gives a wave at which I duck behind the rubbery gray drape hung from a thin cable at the back of the room. Twenty-three. I hear the instructor tidying my station, the splash of clay being dumped into vat, chatter about the storm as I cast off my smock. Listening passively more to the music of the conversation than the sense, I ease out of my jeans, and lean over the wash basin to scrub the stubborn clay from my arms and hands when beneath the water something calls my name. *Aurora. Aurora.* I plunge the handle down, a thump resounding against the walls as it swallows hard. I wait to hear the instructor, the staff's mellow tones joining in as if strummed, before raising the handle again. *Aurora.* The water gushes. *Aurora.* I slam it down. I hear a body in the pipes, recoiling in the tank, and then its voice as it's freed again in a rush. *Aurora.*

"Aurora?" say the fingers sprouting a head of gray curls that part the curtain. "Ray needs to get back. Hurry," the instructor winks, seeing I'm okay before he retreats.

I tear the plastic and tape from my arms, pulling the taut skin red and feeling the crack of blood beneath the bandage as I ball the mass and toss it into the trash in the middle of a wall of supplies. Easels, stacks of paint cans, and large rolls of brown paper are among the disorder which goes unnoticed from the other side of the curtain.

In haste, I slip a black jersey skirt over my hips and wriggle into a peacock green top. There is a taupe crayon lying on the workbench, which I'll use to line my eyes. Toxic perhaps, but they've taken my things and put them in a sharps box. In the flat reflection of a paint lid, I smudge it in before noticing my cracked lips and the bruise on my right clavicle beginning to yellow.

We are late and have to hustle over the paved walk with a shared umbrella, the winds throwing us against each other as we go. When I take hold of Ray's forearm to steady myself, he stops and queerly studies me in the rain. Why does it feel like a reprimand? Why do I feel like I've done something wrong? That rain strikes at my skin then in punishment?

On our arrival, he drops the umbrella in the anteroom and takes my coat with an uneasy smile. We proceed into the main hall, where the patients' rooms are arranged off a great room with a circle of squat burgundy chairs at its center. The psychologists and psychiatrists are off the hall toward the south side.

"You've been reassigned for the morning," a voice calls after us. We're both drenched. When we turn, the water comes off of us like dogs. (Hyperbole. If you could see the water in the light peeling off of us, it would be beauty, and I would be okay for a while, safe in an image.) "Turn around and take the third door on your right."

"But I've been working with Dr. Worden," I gripe and continue although my companion stops.

"This is not up for discussion," says the firm voice of a man then, who looks like your average middle-aged psychologist, plain and bookish in his green tweed jacket and brown flannel slacks, standing in the doorway to his office. He even smells like a psychologist, I notice on approach, an old photograph pressed between the pages of a dying book.

"Dr. Rutch," I say, reading the placard on my way through the door. "I'd really prefer talking to a woman. There are things I can't say in front of you."

"Please come in, Aurora," he says, guiding me in with handshake and a palm on my lower back against which I

44

stiffen. Another man closes us in.

"This is my colleague, Dr. Wolff." Dr. Wolff nods. "We would like to get you started on some medications with the intention of getting you out of here by the end of the month. Now how does that sound?"

"But I was told that wouldn't be necessary."

"Getting out of here? Surely, you can't stay!" he says laughing heartily and gesturing toward the couch at the room's center. I take a seat in the middle, my long hair dripping into my lap. What did sitting in the middle mean? I'm sure they're noting it. I'm sure they are. I run my hands over my scalp to keep my hair from sticking to my head and try to wring out the ends over the floor. Dr. Rutch and Dr. Wolff exchange a look I catch on looking up.

"Considering your history we are convinced it would be malpractice to let you walk out of here in your current state," Dr. Wolff explains in a voice more like a coyote.

"What's my current state?" I retort, betrayed.

"Your evaluation confirms a diagnosis of bipolar disorder, which could easily be helped by a number of drugs." Pathology.

"But therapy was working."

"Granted," says Dr. Rutch, looking toward Dr. Wolff for support, "but it's a slow process."

"And unreliable at that," adds Wolff. I slide back into the taut brown leather sofa, which is so deep that I find myself staring at the scuffed toes of my Mary Janes, where I've skipped a stair or taken a corner too narrowly. It was the thinkers who were clumsy, a history teacher of mine once said, so much in their heads that motors skills were fleeting.

"Hear us out," Dr. Rutch continues. "Doesn't it make sense that if your chemicals are out of whack, it might cause you to think crazy thoughts? Once we bring these chemicals back into alignment, it is possible you needn't do so much work. In other words, you might not need therapy at all in the long-term."

"But I like therapy. It clarifies things for me."

"Perhaps you will respond equally positively to drugs."

"With all due respect gentlemen," I pause, trying to maintain some control, "whatever my chemical composition, it is mine, and I'll deal with it." Why is this happening? "I just need to see Dr. Worden," I say, getting up. "Something happened yesterday in our session and…"

"We're well aware of that, young lady," Dr. Rutch interrupts. "It's all here." He's waving my clinical file, the sudden exposure of which silences me, while motioning for me to take a seat.

"In fact, at one point you were on an antidepressant, which in your own words…" Dr. Wolff supplies, running his index finger down the clipboard as if down my spine. I shudder, and he glances up and then finishes in the same irksome pitch. "Made you 'euphoric'." It yips from him.

"No doubt," concurs his colleague, sensing my aversion I suppose. "It merely fed your manic side, but when paired with a mood stabilizer the effects could be quite powerful. I think you'll find your personality unaltered. Imagine living without debilitating suicidal thoughts."

Shocked by the shift in caregivers, I cannot form a cohesive argument in rebuttal no matter how I try. I have worked so hard to understand this inner world. "But if there are reasons and I can find the source…"

"If you had black boils covering your feet, and I could administer a drug that would make you cancer-free, would you refuse that, too? I'm afraid I cannot allow it," responds Dr. Wolff in termination of the discussion.

WHAT COMES OF THE NIGHT *waking softly on the light, a gift lifting its wings toward you in which you see enough to incite the mind to wonder, to believe. Here before you an angel, a god moving its hands in the light. And here beauty is. Know that it witnesses you, that you are not alone. Know that you were chosen for this, that there is a reason for restlessness, a reason for discontent. It is spirit longing; what you are seeking growth, ever in spate.*

A web spun of light and glass lingers in the eaves.

IMAGINATION AND THE DIVINE.

"What if the realm of imagination were a manifestation of the divine and you were destroying that?" I continue at a follow-up session with Dr. Rutch the next day. I have had time to consider my argument.

"When God influences a woman to stab herself, I am willing to take that risk."

"This didn't come from God," I say, lifting my arm, "but from some deep-seeded frustration within. If anything, my spiritual conscience is what saved me."

"Look, crazy manifests in many divine ways from tainted Kool-Aid to jihad. That your last doctor humored you in these discussions is the primary reason for your reassignment." Saying this he takes a cursory look at my bandages and frowns. "Once we've stabilized your Lithium levels and gotten you started on an antidepressant, I think you'll find this a moot point. There are other ways of seeking God."

I start at the mention of the reassignment. "But that's just it, Dr. Rutch, these are the ways meant for me. I'm the one being plagued with dark thoughts. I'm the one being visited, if that's what these visions are. And if they are just hallucinations, then my body is manifesting them for a reason. Regardless, putting me on drugs only takes away my reason to live."

"How so, Aurora?" Dr. Rutch listens from beyond a low hedge. I know from his condescending tone and relaxed posture, his left ankle turned up on the knee, that I've approached the subject incorrectly. Is it too late to begin again? I take a deep breath, clearing the space.

"I'm not uneducated on the subject, Dr. Rutch. I minored in psychology, and I've recorded my moods in poetry since I was thirteen." I hope he won't find me prating and dull. "You're familiar no doubt with Kay Redfield Jamison. In addition to her brilliant study on the artistic temperament and its role in the creative process, which, incidentally, I discovered on my last hospital visit, I've also read her memoir and in it her argument for pharmacological treatment. In fact, I recognize myself and my argument against it in many of her examples."

He stops massaging his ankle and cocks his head to the side.

"Although at times I concede drugs would be easier," I continue, "it is against my better judgment to give in. I've come too far in my knowledge of self and in my understanding of mind."

"Do you realize how close you came to severing an artery?"

I nod, looking down at the purple appendage in my lap. "What if I were on the verge of discovering what would change this forever?"

"And if it is merely acausal and you've risked your life because your mind was tricked by a disease?" By its very nature the disorder persuades the individual into hubris at times, into believing he or she is chosen to deliver the world. Because he cannot allow himself to be dissuaded, he reverts to the factual. "I don't think you understand how critical your situation is," he goes on. "That you take your treatment seriously enough to familiarize yourself with its literature, I can appreciate. But according to your hospital records you were admitted to the ER only 5 months ago with a laceration to the wrist that could have cost your life. Why they did not incarcerate you then, I should like to find out, for I'm guessing it was also self-inflicted." He raises his eyebrows questioningly, and I challenge his gaze although my cheeks flush hot. "This thing is progressive. I trust with a bit of honesty you would admit that." I'm touching each finger of my left hand to my thumb: forefinger middle ring pinky pinky ring middle forefinger. Then quicker in succession. "If you need a metaphor to relate to it's a slippery animal that you've chosen to play with. Like heart disease or lung cancer, it will kill you."

"Now you sound like your cohort, who—where is he by the way?" I ask, departing from the current theme *ring pinky pinky ring middle* and casting a glance around the room. The doctor eyes my hand with its seemingly autonomous mission.

"I mean to scare you," he adds in a rebuking tone *middle ring pinky* to which he rises. "I'm afraid our session has ended. We'll speak again on Thursday."

Because it has never been put to me so bluntly before, I can't stop thinking about the progressive nature of this thing. What if I *have* been duped? What if something does have control of my mind and is forcing this argument out of a death wish? It wouldn't be the first time. But the idea of that right now seems more far-fetched than any I've proposed. I feel healthy, honestly, and focused like I haven't been for some time. Besides, the usurpation of mind is preceded by something, always, and I can get myself out of it. A past therapist taught me that. I need only to pay attention to my moods and when I notice them plummeting to stop and trace the descent back to its source in the external trigger. This is not new to me and, contrary to Dr. Rutch's beliefs, I know the disorder to be manageable in this way. For what is disorder when it is understood? It is ordered and healed. Although my success with it varies, there is always a catalyst however small, and then a succession of events tainted by the first until I'm wrapped in their dark layers and can't see beyond. Reason is tipped into the underside of conscious and all is lost but the impulse to escape. Curiously, the mania, too, stems from here, as if the emotion were so dark that it transmuted into brightness, in the breaking off that everything screams into life.

Yet one doesn't go mad while holding on. What is scaring me is that I also know the places where coming back is not so easy; where a lifeline has to be slung from an external source, for chaos has taken over the core. There is a loss of self, a loss of center. What when the mind slips from one reality to another? What when what pleased me yesterday is today a banal thing? 'Which of the me's is me?' as Jamison put it.

That parts of the self live lives we are not privy to. I've seen it. I've willed it. It is. Suddenly one speaks from the corner and my reality is erased. I am something else, a particle disappearing, reappearing. When this is the world in which I find myself, intelligence plays no role but in analysis after the fact. I am slung into a scene I do not recognize. If I can figure out how I've gotten here; if I can be honest enough within... If I can somehow find a lifeline in time and trace it back to its source, to the moment of derailment, everything rights itself and stabilizes, and I'm okay. But I need to be in my own head to do this. Un-medicated. As capricious as it is sometimes I need to remain if I am ever to find the way out for good. And so an object in motion remains in motion; the proclivity toward hopelessness and despair, toward absence and abandonment although faint at times, remained.

HARBINGERS. The pendulum sweeps from ground to ground, through polarities where wisdom speaks and knowledge itself is silent.

When darkness draws near, visions become harbingers of the plane of light. I am not alone. Before me on the opposing wall, two spiders the size of my hands dangle from a single thread, one spinning the other into existence, one born of the other, both born of light. The vision recedes and the room becomes as it was before they slipped through. Another realm consummates this realm. Call it what you will, I commune with something.

Something calls, something speaks. Even as the city in perfect opacity and fortitude presents itself in concrete evidence, I slide beneath its walls to a parallel plane. I am its river and sea, a confluence of movement and metaphor.

ASCENSION.

Nor is standing before me, the hospital lighting casting a sheen over his wounds so that they glow violent purple; his skin in contrast holds out white like a badge. I look down at my own hands and at the bandage gray with clay.

"How is it we come to house demons?" I ask. "That there is a hand beneath my hand holding a knife to my heart? That something hazes me for weakness that is not myself as much as I am not myself. And what am I without this thing, without what drags in me, then lifts and suspends? When will it ever stop plaguing me?" I've been started on a low level of lithium, and my lips are parchment against my paper tongue. "It promises only when my life is in a state of balance, which requires stagnancy, doesn't it? In stagnancy there is no growth. So I suppose the demons, the unrest in the mind, by this rationale, are agents of growth." I stop, expecting that he's stopped listening.

"Go on," he says. I'm balancing myself on the bed's edge on the rickety metal frame.

"There is something in the instability, a reason for it that I'll never find out, not like this. Salt in my head and they're dying. Why does this feel like giving up?" The tile is cold beneath my feet, burnished white with dendritic black streaked through. I want to put my chest to it. I want to feel cold patch the ragged hole.

"My theory?" he says, settling beside me. "A certain level of ascension often finds us bipolar. At extreme states the body reaches a state of ecstasy in which knowledge is gleaned in the form of energies. However uncomfortable to sustain, these states allow us a higher rate of spiritual growth. For most maintaining a normal life is nearly impossible, as I gather you've experienced."

"Yes, and what of the ones who don't make it?" I ask, raising my eyes. "The suicides?"

"I'm afraid I'm precluded from knowledge of an afterlife, not being dead." He brushes a hand across my cheek, and I smile before going on.

"We tend to think we're erased when we die, or born again without prior knowledge of what we've lived, but what if it did in fact inform us? What if this knowledge came from future as well as past for time were conflated, non-structured? What if instead of erasing the self in this equation, we erased time? What if she existed within us as a guide, a voice of what we'd become? These are the things I want to explore. Instead I'm marching around stacking papers, collecting data into files, and trying to pretend I'm not numb."

"You're just misplaced," he says as I lean toward him and then ease myself to the floor. My pantlegs are long and scuffed with dirt below the heel. *Help me.* "What happens in mania, Aurora? You're God-sent; invincible, a pendulum loose from the frame, what longs to be full of itself and free from what hampers and contains. Here is possibility and flight. Here you're touched gold with a thousand dreams to be realized."

"But how long, Nor, until something breaks in me? Until the shank disassembles, jilting the cage. How long until the writhe, the rub of callus envelops the head? How long until I am a sack emptied on a cart of sacks? How long until I see the reality in nothing? And which of the realities when there is nothing to bridge them, and I surface so far from myself I may never return?"

"I don't know, Aurora," he confesses. "This thing was slung on me. Wings. Do you know what it is to have the might to fly? But to be slung, to be nothing but what is sent?"

There are conversations within her that wallow in silence. Watching her slip her hands over the floor it becomes clear to him they are burning out. It is why the light has breached her. There is wisdom about her that comes from her reverence for life, for all things but herself. Whereas he understands the rage she speaks of as something to turn outward, against the perpetrator against the oppressor, he guesses to Aurora this is self. How has she become the hunted?

THE SHADOW ONES. We are the shadow ones; light comes of our need to create: a geometric shift, an intricate lantern hung on my waking. A doorframe stitched in thread perhaps portends something. Trauma comes and webs of light and glass span the rafters. The cathedral ceiling is aglow in an intricate divinely rendered pattern blinking cannot disperse.

In hiatus I ask for its return. Let there be something good of a mind that does not sleep but rattles on in all tedium, dumbing itself, shutting itself down, a mind that culls through fear, a mind that torments mind that it might survive. At times the mouth empties in stones, an inarticulate mass spilling before me that I cannot but observe.

CROUCH THREAT.

"I don't wish to hear what is wrong with me anymore; that is the source of this madness. Affirm what is. Observe me in awe, but do not hamper what you don't understand," I say to Dr. Rutch on his suggestion they increase my medications. Being with Nor has stirred things within me. What if he were gone because of them?

"You are a threat to yourself and the world. Look at what you shared with me. You said you understood what it was to kill. You were out of control; it will happen again. Of that you can be guaranteed."

"Only if I subscribe to your theories." He stares at me dumbly, his escalating impatience apparent as he picks at the splintered edge of the large oak desk which he sits behind and waits for the explanation that will inexorably follow. "Self-fulfilling prophesy, Dr. Rutch."

Almost audibly, his rebuttal swells on the back of his tongue.

"Picture a bird," I proceed, "a tall white bird on long black legs, a whooping crane. You enter its cage unbidden and there before you it folds its scarlet crowned head down its ivory back, slides gracefully its long beak along its pristine wings. Its legs collapse beneath it, and it falls before you in obeisance. This is a threat. Try to understand that."

"A threat."

"Yes, how a threat might look like genuflection."

Dr. Rutch sighs.

"Do not blink and take no further step, for its beak, now

a weapon, draws blood from the hands you lift in shield."

"Okay, so threat can be disguised."

"No. Not so much disguised as indifferent to your interpretations. Here, vulnerability bows toward its opponent with all the wisdom of the feminine divine. For ages our strength has been misinterpreted, misunderstood, and misled. That movement downward, that seeming display of relinquishment and concession belies a connection with the inner divinity, the source of wisdom and craft; it is here that we are beyond reproach, for wisdom harbors no fear. This is the true power of femininity; it forgets not that we are powerful creators within a mysterious world; it forgets not that this world exists within us as much as we exist within the world; it considers everything for it is in touch with all that is; its wisdom is its craft."

What sort of world would it be that took heed?

Later in my room, however, in the silence of alone, the helm will shift, and I will feel the sense of exposure in what I've shared. The berating one will rise, the blackbird I hold within, scourging me for my ignorance. Then the image of the bird will become wicked: the story of my life, the innocent beauty entering the cage where the regal one bows and then ravages. He has conjured wings as a lure; he has conjured a victim's stance so that in him I see myself: obsequious wench, my hand torn and guilty, bleeding in stark winter light, my skin wind-worn white. The boned beak chipped where the man had smashed it.

How do we discard where we've been? Why would the world I have written choose such vile imagery? And why must reality either shine or rust?

I tire of my thoughts and set my head down on my pillow as gray stones spill onto a strand.

VOLATILE TEMPERAMENT.

"Not to be cantankerous, but how much sense does it really make treating a volatile temperament with such a sensitive drug?" I begin the next day.

"Excuse me. I'm afraid I fail to see your point."

"Lithium levels need to be carefully monitored, right?"

He nods.

"This responsibility lies with the bipolar patient in the end. In the end, it is she who must remember to take her meds at the right time and so maintain the proper blood levels."

"Of course," Dr. Rutch says, with a reassuring grin. "Once you start to feel better it becomes routine."

"Yet the whole concept ignores a fundamental principle of the disorder, the proclivity toward polar extremes. It is as if you've set her atop a crag, fed a rope into her hand and said, now you can either remain on the headland where everything is predictable and safe or plunge from this height and sail off over the ocean like a bird before drowning in its depths."

Dr. Rutch chuckles. "Naturally you'd opt for the latter."

"That's where I get to live," I say. "Our emotional states affirm our existence. We forget the plodding sickness that wrenches the core, though even that strokes a sweet note inside. This is life."

"A clear reliable mind and you'd trade it for sickness? It is only that you haven't known it yet."

"Oh but I have, and my mind is quite reliable. It only

becomes virulent when I act against the self."

"Are we really going to have this conversation again?"

"I would just like you to hear me out, because it seems to me absurd. Every medication they've ever put me on I've used as a jumping off point to plunge straight into a depressive episode."

"I've explained before, the meds were wrongly prescribed. Bipolar disorder is often indistinguishable from unipolar in the onset of a depressive episode. As our only screening to date consists of a questionnaire, misdiagnosis at the early stages can occur. You were tipped into mania. Had they administered the antidepressant in combination with a mood stabilizer, perhaps you wouldn't have felt compelled to jump off an artificial height. You see, once you're stabilized, such self-destructive thoughts simply won't occur to you anymore."

"But I don't want to be droned. It's the chicken and the egg again, Dr. Rutch. And don't you know they've proven the chicken came first?"

"What?" he asks, abandoning all etiquette.

"They've discovered a protein in the egg shell that can only be produced by the chicken. If you'll allow, I think the implications are quite clear: I've spawned the illness."

He gawks incredulously. Where will this end? "Art therapy, Aurora. Draw an F-ing diagram! Finger-paint the damn chicken, but give this a chance. That's all I ask."

"Something in my mind has created this disorder in response to outer stimuli. These brain patterns you've observed are only symptomatic. They don't dictate madness any more than a terrible childhood dictates a miserable adulthood. Just as symptoms are alterable, so are the brain wirings that manifest."

"I will not withdraw the order."

"I didn't expect you to. I just want to be included in the conversation."

"Prove then that it's true, if you think you can alter the chemical makeup of the brain. Not only I, but all of science will be happy to include you in such discourse. Until then…" he says dismissively.

"I don't think you respect the delicacy of my efforts."

"There you're wrong. It is by its very nature impossible. You're conducting research with a faulty instrument. Furthermore, your scientist's mad!"

"Go ahead, doc, laugh. I don't find it amusing. I've put too much into this. There's too much at stake."

"I see," he says, jotting some notes into the black folder spread at his knees. 'Delusional' I imagine. "Do you think you're the first to propose some cockamamie idea in here?" he asks with a guffaw, his nose turning quite red, and I tire of talking to him altogether. "Exaggerations of grandeur, the god complex, the belief that anything is possible."

"Anything *is* possible," I mumble under my breath while he shifts in his chair and tugs his pant legs down in an agitated fashion. Properly taking his seat again, he continues quite animatedly rattling off a list.

"Within the next five years a new and truly benign energy source will emerge out of nowhere, as prolific as oxygen, one of your colleagues assured me before heading off to Nairobi as part of 'God's plan'. He's left behind four children under the deranged illusion that he is ultimately securing their future."

"What's in Nairobi?"

"That is neither here nor there. He's hurt a lot of people."

"But if it's his calling, and he is part of a brighter future."

"Oh yes, but why stop there when the 2nd earth will emerge on a parallel plane through which travel will be possible through the development of the 7th sense, a sense that is strengthened by gaming and that combines the esoteric principles of astral travel with computer technology."

"Wild! Is one of your patients working on this?"

He rolls his eyes. "2012 bullshit is what this is. The wave of the future, wave of the future, wave of the future."

I laugh, transported to the end of The Aviator. "Good film."

"Yeah, well, Hughes was nuttier than a fruitcake."

"But a creative genius."

"Look, Aurora, our session has ended. Be a good patient and take the drugs."

"Of course, Dr. Rutch. Your chart should show I already have."

"Thank you," he says exhaustedly sinking down into the brown tufted chair. "Wave of the future," he whispers again as I close the door. My petulance infuriates him.

DIAGNOSES.

What sleeps in the dark recesses of mind has knowledge of what transpires without consciously knowing the motivations or mindset. In unconscious it knows only what is implicit. There is a gap in the reel and just how trenchant this gap defines the extent of damage and recalls the disorder. Many times the patient fits not only one of the definitions within the Diagnostic and Statistical Manual of Mental Disorders (DSM), but two or three at any given time. Although Aurora has been diagnosed with bipolar and borderline personality disorders, these are gradients of another, these manifestations of other selves. How easily the personality breaks off at our intention. There are times when the severity breaches the cusp of multiple personality. She's acculturated herself to the divided mind. But the DSM is a tool, neither definitive nor complete. It offers us patterns, a way in, a structure for understanding, but that is all, and the crone is beside herself in this room.

FAELAN. INSIDE WINTER.

Pervasive gray, and the morning wears the face of erasure, a sponge run through with silt and wrung out over the sky. The cards slip from the dreamer's hands. Water ticks in the gutter, and a voice is heard in the wall calling out my name. Over the water it calls, and it calls, and I strain my ears for its words. It is not real, I tell myself. It is the water in the drain, but it doesn't let up though I slip beneath my pillow and clench it tightly to my ears.

Are you a wraith, it seems to be saying. And closer still, "Aurora, are you a wraith?"

The voice becomes familiar then. Lifting the pillow, I feel his breath before I see Faelen crouching over me. Like Nor, there are some we meet on another level, inviting immediate closeness. He extends his body toward me, touching to affirm my presence, absorbed by something very real to him that I can't see. If we are caught, I cannot imagine the trouble it'd bring.

"What is it, Faelen? What is it?" I whisper as he flings himself hard against my side like a heavy animal. His hip pokes into my thigh.

"Get them out of me."

Is it the same for him? He knows. He must, and yet I don't know how to do this for someone else. I don't know how to enter him, to find the rooms of things he hides. I pull the cover down and set a hand tentatively on his side, which he absently shirks off.

Laughter is spilling in tears down his face.

"Get them out of me," he cries again, shoving his cold feet beneath my rump. His hands are at the base of his scalp, leaking out in creatures, sickly white on bent limb, thumbing their way down his forearms.

"They're part of you Faelen." I'm saying this to myself.

"They want me decimated."

"They're part of you."

A crescendo of voices fills the hall. Someone knocks on the door, and I stash him beneath the bed before a head appears with the flick of the light. A bob swings into the doorway. A thick hand wicks a strand of hair away, curling it behind a carrot-pink ear.

"Is Faelen with you?"

"Faelen?" I ask dumbly, rubbing my eyes, my voice a flat contrast to hers.

She gives a cursory glance around the room before responding, "All right, hon. Breakfast in 8 minutes." The door clicks shut.

Faelan has removed his top I notice on hanging over the side of the bed. He is slender and bony and his expression has returned to glum, which he wears rather wraithlike in the mess of brown hair. He is frightened. Whatever has been stirred in his sessions causes his body to tremor and his face to pale. I have to get him out of here.

"Fae," I whisper, but his face is blank. Think, Aurora, think. How does the external get in? A lifeline slung from the outside. I reach one of his arms, but he jerks it away, slamming against the springs of the bed. The inner hold is too strong; I've become a pawn in the mind's game, one of the demons sent to haul him off.

I try to imagine the landscape, what it would look like within. Meanwhile he's screeching like a bird, and it's hurting my heart; his cry resonating against the springs, reverberating beneath, and forcing me to collapse onto his body to silence him. I slip my hand quietly over his mouth.

In response, the room shudders and expands until it spans a stretch of earth. The ground is filled with hoarfrost, great plates of ice sheeting the lake that opens out before me. There is another cry from the center where waters spill into wood, there where Faelan weeps and staggers toward the trees, a boy following his uncle on a hunt. A six-year-old with a shaggy mop of hair and plaid flannel shirt, he looks a smaller version of the man, rifle trailing through the leaves, seduced with adventure. They plod on, their clothes steeped in deer piss, their boots drenched in mud.

In the autumn light that leaks from the horizon how beautifully sterile it all seems, how ordered and clean in the pink light leaking out of the morning, swans with their heads perpetually bent into the frozen water and birds that fly up from the backs of black trees. It is tragedy and the heart latches on and understands it is this connecting us, this that makes us wild. This that raises its red tongue to the sky and cries *Stop*. All I can do here is watch and it is like watching myself as he falls and a broken thing falls from the sky, for there touching down in the wavering light is a bare-legged angel, his wings half unfurled, stark against the winter sky's sun-weak radiance. A howl breaks from the woods. Winter stretches itself across the back, its cold dragged as I'm dragged across snow-encrusted ice and pulled into the sky in the angel's arms. I am flying, dangling, with no will of my own, then dropped where the leaves are golden brown and ice-glazed, where Faelan huddles in a den at the base of an oak.

An extended hand replaces the uncle's hand, and Faelan latches on as the dark-winged angel braces himself against the boy's body. When Nor speaks, it is a heavy string against the silent landscape. "I am the alpha and omega," he says. What he means is there's no end to this.

There is the sound of water exhaling its hoar into the bare branches of trees, a cacophony at the mergence of realm. Wings push through the branches at my back; piles of snow, shaken from the trees, stomp to the ground. In the falling there is movement as if beneath me, a swell of wave then a hand around my waist. A face in my hand.

Aurora?

His grey eyes glisten in fear. About me hang branches,

resplendent in the fading light. I am the grief god holding the boy's face in my hand, holding him to stillness, holding him until he relinquishes all, until his soft eyes slip away under a cursed thing.

It helps that it is sleeting, that there is movement without and pattering. The illusion is I've conspired with the gods for things that nothing earthly knows of. It is the words placed in the lover's mouth for you. He knows not what he has said, perhaps enchanted, perhaps the gods have thickened him, spun the hair gold. Or perhaps I have done this. What does it matter but that something is created that is or is not real. What is reality but shape-shifting? There are places where the womb strains to recover what it has lost. Places where you've achieved this thing called love. Places of two-dimension where ruling is easy, everything dirigible, where the self is a thing easily defined, where it does not split and rot, where it does not abandon.

Lick the metal blood from the corner of your mouth. On the ground before you a boy you don't know. A boy you have never wanted to know in this way, but there he is. He, the weak animal you hold within, the one that allows you to feel shame destroy him *so that we are both his face witnessing shame and that blotting it out. Fear keeps things at a distance. Love is intertwined with pain. No one will ever get this close to us.*

So it is that whether by exhaustion or fear Faelan passes out in the bed of leaves. A gust shakes the bows, and a prattle of voices is heard on the cusp. A door opens. What it coaxes into consciousness opens into the sterile hands of white gloves and leather straps, so that I'm left to the treachery of what I've done.

THE DARK SHADOW stirs in me. It has asked this of me again, and again I respond with a cry so horrific and strained that none on the outside can hear what the inside has done. Fire rages and fevers my torso with red heat. My skin burns. I am ashamed of my lidless eyes and the color I've become.

THE ONES AT THE WINDOW.

Fear manifests on the black stage of the window where faces ascend. It has taken something with it this time, part of me that means absence. I sit with it until its white gloves become the space between my organs, until I am human and frail looking back. I am trying to understand and incorporate everything into the self instead of dividing it out, instead of deeming this part evil or bad. Darkness is shadow; darkness the unknown; darkness the antithesis of light, and so light. It is this dis-ease that plagues me, that causes me to seek, that causes my flight and sometimes stillness. Piles of coarse stones form in the mouth and empty before me onto the sand until I'm standing again before the red moon rising from the back of the horizon, rising so *weit entfernt* it becomes the god's hands touching me into not turning away.

Do not bore into the sand; do not burrow or hide, for this is what you have come for and what has sought you. The boy at your side is in you, pushing away at your flesh, displacing sand from the hole you've hollowed out beneath, and you are turning away like what rolls back in escape, you, the discarded thing, the warm tool. And here he will say apocalypse and here he will say what rises red calls for the end of the world and here he will lift you up and push your head back into the sand and here he will push your face toward the horizon your hair balled in a fist at the back of your head and you will see as you do now the scene unfolding through lidless eyes the fiery light catching a ship and setting it aflame. What turns the body away and what burns the ship are perpetual and cannot be stopped or erased. Look at your body; the sand burns, the scars.

THE OUTSIDE WORLD IS DISTRACTION.

"Aurora."

There is a man at the window with four grown boys not his own. This could be Gabriel, his voice hoarse from smoke and drink.

"What'd you get attacked by a dog?" he asks lightly.

"Something like that," I say. When his arm comes at me, I imagine a fishing knife, dull blade.

"Me, too," he says, coaxing my heart into place.

"Aurora."

I look up to see a nurse practitioner with a clipboard in her hand. The doctor is behind his desk stacking files. When he lowers himself into a chair and tows a drawer from the lower cabinet, a low moan is released into the room at its weight, as if what it contained were so burdensome that it asked me to assess the weight of need. What right do I have to be here and live? And why are there some who would give so much to save us?

"It's not real, Aurora," Dr. Rutch says again. "The darkness that you feel is a malfunction of the brain. When your blood sugar drops and a cantankerous child rages loose, is there meaning in that, too? Eat a cookie." I slip down to the floor as he finishes, imbed my fingertips in the rug and rub my palms across its fibers until it burns. "Your brain needs salt."

What good will it be not to wonder anymore when it feels this is why I have come?

"I see light, Dr. Rutch, and know that it witnesses me and that in that recognition I am made other. Think in terms of the Holy Spirit, what enters us when we allow it to, what blesses us with godlike craft, but remember always what wishes to reveal itself to us must also reveal its antithesis.

"To know the self is to know God," I continue. "In that wish I empowered a force so great that it split in two. The helm shifted as one side grew stronger, then the other in volatile way. The two stood at the window at night drawing figures on the woods' surface. Men came, their intention only to empty fright into vessel, so that when the two returned"—overhead dark wings occlude the moon—"one could swear she saw a tattered edge now to their forms, singed metal radiating from the shoulders."

"I'm afraid I cannot follow."

"What I want comes from hallucination," I explain. "It is not real. God does not speak to me. God does not unveil a golden realm on my waking. God does not coax me forth into a place where all is light and glass. God does not in this way mark me as the chosen one. God does not cast webs across the beams that glimmer in their own light. God does not make his presence known in the form of angel towering above me, its girth spanning the room. God does not tilt a lantern toward my face at night waking me, transporting me to a realm an extension of the internal."

My cracked voice stops, and I look at the man seated before me. I have worn him down in ways he does not understand. His face searches mine for vulnerability, for concession although what he hears in my voice offers none.

"I see an angel," I beseech, "and know not what it illuminates but a spirit within that will not starve. Do you see now how I need these things?"

"Pray," he says, but I don't hear him, for the outside is only façade. Everything has shifted so that I can only hold on within. I don't remember how I got so far away and why the language I speak is misunderstood. What used to be beauty peals like laughter over my broken form. Are there none here that recognize me?

BLACKBIRD. HOUSE OF WINTER.

The girl who enters the room is no longer a child. Her long gray tunic and torn ankle belie innocence. I turn questioningly toward the crone, who redirects my gaze. The girl suffers. One has the sense that she is rotating on an axis a bit off kilter as frost rises from the garb.

"It's the one you shoved in the house. One cannot repress parts of self without having them rear up, emerge with vengeance. You must finish them off."

"What happened to reintegration?" I ask, not trusting this game.

"When one so vehemently and resolutely refuses to respond to her cries for help, I assume she is no longer receptive to therapeutic device. She doesn't trust you."

"Wouldn't this have some sort of grave repercussion?"

"It is like a mercy killing. We feed her the lollipop and watch her drift off."

"But what is it that…?" For the girl contains such beauty.

"It is suffering and you are again romanticizing it. It is not holy, or some high art. The girl suffers. She feels pain. There is no gleaning of wisdom, no power or insight here. Can't you ever learn pragmatism?"

I don't hear her goading, however, for the girl, a cold, gray thing the color of a late winter sky, whisks a piece of hair back from my eyes. *Rescind,* she says, clothes smelling of soot, and when I pull back I wear the gray shadow of a muzzle.

The pillow drains the spleen, the coffer yielding its armor so that I may witness pleurisy, the lungs sopped within, the damp ache of winters long held. The wounded ideals, what's torn inside. Vertigo. What portal is this? Where breath pours through the hollow?

A wave washes in from a northern shore, a brown-green cast flooding over the girl's hands as she tips me back into the water, and my lids shutter closed like a doll. When I open them again, hers shift white like a bird. My face feels pinched where it's touched her, and her clasp tightens on my hand. Cold aches through my fingers, extends through my wrist, traverses the forearm, the shoulder and neck until I find myself petrified; my earlobes ice.

"You are the past I can't reconcile," the girl's voice stung with burn, "the one the students ate limb from limb in the schoolroom."

There is a soft clenching, a bar lifting me by the throat.

"Violence begets violence begets violence begets violence," I hear as a litany hung on a band that keeps slipping around on my neck.

"Kill her and you will stop suffering," says the white witch over the darkness. "You will be free of pernicious memories."

But she is wrong. Through the thick fluid glass of the bird's eyes something pierces, perceiving what longs to be nurtured as if it were weak. She could kill, this bird that takes hold of my hand. A cold, gray thing. The bird is whispering this in my ear in fact.

What will you do? the whisper asks. *Nothing*, it answers, its cheeks thick slabs of flesh crowding my mouth. The one within burns. Whatever is outside incites her. How beautifully what she's written finds its way to the world. Nothing can touch this.

Winter is closed, the chest a sieve, baleen drawn of emptiness, a frozen house, the floorboards lain bare, while I remain conscious within, here in winter's coffer, divided from the one at the helm.

Masked ones spill into the garden. Light sieves through the screen into yard.

PARALLEL UNIVERSES.

"The wise voice within gleans knowledge in ways unknown to us. We are continuously bombarded with symbols and signs. If we have learned somewhere to ignore them, it is in this life," Nor says seriously. "But something deeper in us knows. Play the game of life aware. Know you are guided by knowledge that transcends time and space. Know that your curiosity and emotional needs draw roots that draw us down and ask to be tended. Meet love aware. Be ready to end things when the all-knowing voice says you have no future here; he only hurts you. Isn't it foolish to proceed? To love on?"

"In theory, yes. But what when he's still mine? He's been given to me. What when I have to get through this; what when I'm meant to be changed? Could it be that leaving is a form of escapism here?"

"You're rationalizing when you know the inevitability of the situation."

"Do I? If I take a step to the left everything shifts. Another step and what you foresee fades. It's not so linear. The closer I get to myself the more the outside confirms the changes."

"You're rationalizing," Nor says again more quietly.

"What if we allow for parallel universes? The idea that anything you can possibly imagine has already occurred? The whole damned thing becomes a choose-your-own adventure. Can you imagine pulling things toward you by the attention that you give, investing them with energy intentionally?

That's empowerment. What would this look like? We are the cosmos pulling and repelling, shifting and attracting on a smaller scale but a more rapid rate. What informs the shifting energies but instability? The more imbalanced, the quicker the transformation. Which we might then expand to conclude makes us more godlike for it is creative and what is God but the ultimate creator, which is why the universe is in constant flux and why those with emotional disorders are closer to God."

"You cannot change him," he warns.

CONTROL.

"If you can explain everything, then why are you here?" Dr. Rutch wants to know as he picks aggressively at the edge of his desk.

"Creative people have less ability to…"

"Enough!"

"Filter experience," I finish.

"What do you have, a blog you've abandoned since your incarceration? For God's sake, Aurora. In plain English. I asked you a question. Why are you here?"

"Because I hate my life."

"Finally," he says and stops picking. "Go on."

"Look at me, Dr. Rutch. All I control is killing this thing." I hold up the arm dressed in a constrictive white net. It is a swollen, bulbous, eggplant colored thing. "I fucked up and I can't get back," I say, lowering it carefully into my lap.

"Get back where?"

"Back where I stop trying to destroy what I am because it doesn't have a place in the world." An infuriated growl causes him to ease back in his chair. "I don't feel good. Don't you see? And I'm not good at this. I keep doing things that I hate myself for."

"What things, Aurora? What things do you do? This with the boy?" Receiving no answer, he lets me brood for a while.

My palms are wet. When I wipe them on my pant legs, a glister surfaces immediately. I try not to look at him watching me as I hold them to my face and blow. "What if everything about you were right, but your environment were wrong?" I wipe my hands again and then place them on my lap palms up. "What if you weren't meant to be changed, but it? So you don't fit. What if there were some so necessary to the evolution of the world that the universe made it virtually impossible for them to fit in with the world as it is, to pursue a mundane existence? What if that universe descended them into madness if they tried?"

He rolls his eyes, yet encourages me to continue. "What is mundane to you?"

"This. What I'm doing. A monkey could be so successful. I work in a frickin' tax office," I say with disgust. "Data entry, Dr. Rutch. It's mindless, so that I can write in the off-hours, so that I can figure this out from within. There's something in the darkness, a being inside that wants me dead, and there are answers if I could just stay down long enough, if I could just remain long enough within. To know the self is to know God," I say, with a glance to my glistering hands. "I'm not crazy," I lift them and blow again. "I'm beginning to believe when we've been driven from our destiny path, or whatever you want to call it, barriers are erected in order to redirect us. Some of us were sent to change the world. It becomes, therefore, impossible to lead a normal life with everything bucking and rearing up in resistance when we stray into the 9-to-5. Art is not meant to be marginalized; philosophy is a valuable thing, so that everything within hardens against the banal until we can no longer go on doing what we've done." I pause. "You asked why I'm here. This is why. Because I can't do it anymore. The parts of me that are dying are lashing out. This was a surprise," I say, raising my arm again.

"What do you mean a surprise? You said you saw yourself doing it before you ever reached for the knife."

"As much as I saw myself doing it, I guess I dismissed it as a suicide plot, an escapist coping device. The scene that played out in my head merely ameliorated my situation: there was a way out. I don't know how we understand these things. I was doing it in my head. In my head it was clearly me standing at the cutting board stabbing my arm. It made me feel crazy; unique in a way the world wasn't recognizing. Then it happened, and I felt the perfect choreography of laying my arm on the cutting board, unsheathing the knife from the block. How easily everything proceeded, as if it had already been done.

"What followed, of course, I hadn't imagined. How killing a thing might feel and how scared I'd be of dying." I curl my legs into my lap, brush a wick of hair aside, and sit up. Nor would hold me, I say to myself, but I'm not meant to be held. "What I am just now starting to see is that maybe visualizing brought this into existence. Maybe what I'd seen as prescience was just that. My intrigue drew it, but it was I who accepted what I would become. Each time the scene played itself out, and the deviant me cracked a smile, I was strengthening it. Maybe prescience has a mission: to inform us that we might choose another path. Maybe it is like I was warning myself, or God was saying through me, turn around. Only no one was really saying anything. There was no judgment. I could just choose..."

"Interesting conclusion."

"It's nothing new. If we don't control the mind, it turns to darkness. Some Buddhist aphorism. But instead of heeding the warning, instead of turning around, I was fascinated. I liked it, the idea that I was so fucked up as to take a knife to my arm. It fed something in me, something it was drawing on, so that my desire was bringing it closer."

Visualize, Dr. Rutch had told a client recently, a receiver who'd lost confidence in his game. *See the ball against the sky, feel the leather in your hands, your legs vigorously beating the ground* until this young man was virtually completing every pass.

"So would you like to know what I'm conjuring now?" I ask, breaking him out of his thoughts. "It is how I know you're right about a few things." I smile, and he returns my smile touched with pride.

"I'm right about a lot of things. Just what did you have in mind?"

"The progressive nature of this disorder. In the next vision the knife is through my heart. I don't think I survive,"

I say gravely. "And frankly, Dr. Rutch, this time I'm scared."

He shifts in his chair uncomfortably. "You, you have this vision now."

"Just yesterday for the first time. But now that I take it for warning, I am no longer prey."

"Aurora, and I trust an honest answer here, are you planning to kill yourself?"

"No. That's why I'm scared. It's like if I continue like this though, it is inevitable."

"But it is *your* mind and you do control it. Haven't you just asserted this?"

"That's where you're wrong. A week ago I was on automatic pilot. Something flew me through that scene as if it walked the mind. I was unhappy with my life, yes, frustrated, yes, but in control I thought. Controlling what little I could and trying to fix things, trying to heal from all the shit I'd been through." I stop abruptly, cradling my arm and leaning my head back against the sofa.

"Tell me about that." He looks at the clock. We've gone over in session, but he's damned if he's going to release me having made such headway.

"I'm tired."

"Then for my peace of mind, Aurora, if you are no longer prey as you so colorfully put it, how will you defeat the inevitable this time?"

I take a deep breath. "With awareness and intent. I didn't know what it was before. I saw it as augur, what would come to pass independent of my actions."

"How do you know this time will be different?"

"Because we are not meant to live like that anymore. We are not passive animals. I've experienced enough to know how dangerous such thinking can be. And I've had a revelation of sorts."

"Then why the vision, if I might ask?"

"Unfortunately I'm still wrestling old demons. Cognition is one thing, but demons die hard. All that I've conjured has been set in motion, and these patterns I've created, these addictions I've fed, go on. That's why I'm here."

Apparently, my answer mollifies him. "Get some rest. And Aurora"—I turn, my hand on the door—"keep taking your meds. I don't often say this, but I'm rooting for you." He looks like he wants to hug me but settles for knocking me gently on the arm.

I laugh. "Thanks, Dr. Rutch."

THE BOY WHO DOESN'T BATHE. *No one notices the boy slip off. No one sees how he makes the reeds stand down across the marsh. No one sees the rocks he crushes into his hands after the beatings, or the neighborhood girl he befriends; the hair he cuts and scatters into the water; the snake cruelly slung over a tree trunk and duck taped there to die like some stunted limb the girl watches him cut down; the paper dolls and leaves which he burns over a rock; the field mice caught and strung on a spit, still alive. He'll burn their feet, feigning sorrow. But no one will see this. He will simply be the boy who doesn't bathe.*

WHAT I SHOULDN'T HAVE TOLD HIM.

There is a moon with a message for you, but you don't know this yet. You see only her pageantry over low hills dusted in snow as she holds a red lantern to the sky and all is cast in sanguine glow. The snow covered clearing around your building, a flat concrete construction, housing three apartments including your own, opens into an edge of woods, sparse now in its nakedness. Warm yellow light shines from the windows of a home in the distance. All is hushed.

On the other line absence, and the heart holds a yellow thread. It waits and tries again. No answer from the darkness at the other end, and amid the scenarios spun of a panicked mind comes a stark knowing: you are not alone. You have done something terribly wrong in trusting. Go outside. Breathe in, and cold slices you still.

I'm coming home, Aurora, he'd said, meaning what? To God? To you? You'd know him only 14 days. He'd called the hotline wanting to kill himself, had the plan fast-laid, a motorcycle borrowed from a friend and a wire cable thin enough to slice his neck. He'd just been laid off as technician at a chemical plant. Once he'd secured the cable to a concrete wall at the site, fastened the other end around his neck, and given himself enough line to get up to about 65— 550 feet give or take, according to the article he'd read online—death would be imminent. He'd shared this with you along with how he'd watched his head roll into a ditch off the roadside, the wind-swept hair and parched lips as if he'd ridden for miles. Who knows, maybe on that day he would ride for miles, he'd said, but you didn't understand. And there he is before you, standing in the yard in a green t-shirt and beige cords in the dead of winter. He sees you in the window, and the thread falls from your heart. Pick up the phone. Where is he? Somewhere behind the trees. No answer. A rap at the front door.

"Just wanted to let you know Route 4's a mess, if you're going out." It's Harry from the house across the way, smoothing the hood of his unruly parka and stomping the snow off his boots before he takes a quick step inside. His car idles in your driveway. How could you have missed him pulling in? You lean out and his wife, Glenda, waves a mitted hand out the car window. You wave back. The windshield wipers eke across the glass, slowly deliberately, dragging air and a dusting of flakes. "Tractor trailer off the side. They're just now pullin' him out. Could take a while."

"Thanks," you say. "Hey, Marvin's coming by on Tuesday. He wanted to know if you'd go halves on what he's got out there." You cast a glance toward the tarp-faced shed. "I told him you'd had enough wood what with all the bark beetles this year. That he should try Ted, but I didn't have his number."

Harry chuckles. "Yup. I'll give him a call. Got a package from Frederick's of Hollywood the other day. Don't know what that was about."

"Who did? Ted?" you ask. Harry's the 'neighborhood' gossip, the neighborhood having a 35-mile radius. You met him when you moved off campus in your third year. He welcomed you with a four-pound sack of venison and a sack of homegrown. You don't eat deer meat.

"Yut. I saw it delivered and went over to see if maybe it was something he didn't want left out. Heh, heh. Ever seen him with a woman?"

You shake your head, scrutinizing a line of trees. "No, me either," you say distractedly. "Hey listen," you pull him in so closely you smell the seared ends of his whiskers, acid in the breath mingling with frost. "You didn't happen to see anyone when you pulled up, did you?"

"Just that damned black bear. Might be in need of a bed-time story." He motions for the trigger of a gun. "Hope it ain't rabid."

"Yeah, okay," you say, backing up.

"So, I've got to get back now. We're heading over to the Beaumont's."

"Thanks again for the warning," you say although you hadn't intended to go out.

"Yut," he says with the wave of a thickly mitted hand.

You watch him crunch over the path along the building, then wave again to Glenda, who has cleared a peephole in the fogged up windshield. You look out over the street where a pile of felled trees has been lying since fall. The landowner should have had them incinerated according to county regulation, but there they lie contaminating yet another crop of trees with bark beetle larvae the color of pallid skin. If you stand in the lawn, you can hear their red mouths feeding at the succulent core, gnawing assiduously away at the beauty that surrounds you.

A toot of horn as their car backs up, and you wave again, glancing again at the snow-bedecked trees, the moon bundled tightly in a thick yarn of clouds. You shut the door and set the lock. Maybe it was your imagination. In the living room, you stop to slip a scrap of paper in the book you'd flopped open on the couch. As you continue into the kitchen, your eyes fall on the glass door at the back. In the second pane the figure of a man watches you, snow on the porch casting light from behind. Your heart leaps against your throat as he taps at the glass.

The first night he called, you weren't able to sleep. Most of your calls at the hotline were cries for help, people who needed to hear a human voice at the other end. You listened. It's not what one would imagine. Even for those who had been there before, few calls were terribly intimate. You thought a vein would be shared. You thought the cry would open in you. You romanticized the beauty of the moment, thought it would be easy to open into raw pain, easy to provide an anodyne. Most ask so little of others, you thought. But suicides are a highly manipulative, morbid, and malignant bunch, and Victor was no different except that you took him home with you in the way that you feared for him.

When he called the next night, there was less than an hour left to your shift. His voice scraped pain from some abyss. There was something he had to tell you. You had to be the one. At midnight, you should have given the call to someone else, but you couldn't. By chance, he'd gotten you; you had no extensions. When he said you could help him and God knew this, you believed and gave him your number at home. It was against every bit of sense in your head and every employee regulation.

You flick on the light in the hall and approach the figure now lit. He looks younger than you'd imagined. "Victor?" you say, tugging the door free from the ice at its base. It hops up in its track, and he steps forward into the house, trembling. You know it's him, snow beading up in his sandy-colored hair, skin red with cold at the hands and cheeks, hazel eyes glinting as you yank the door again past the ice.

"Damn you're beau-ti-ful," he says, through chattering teeth, and there is sweetness in his visage in which you see the same. He leans in awkwardly, taking your hands and pressing a kiss hard on your cheek. Below his right eye a protrusion disfigures him like a mask the mind busies itself with. You are stunned by this and the frigid posture of his claw-like hands.

"Thanks," you say, cautiously retracting your hands and turning to grab a blanket off the couch. "Where's your coat?" With the wind-chill it's 13 below.

"My car." You casually drape the fleece over his arms, for he's holding them outstretched, harmlessly boy-like.

"Then where's your car?" you ask as he eventually shakes it over his shoulders like a cape.

"Back at the gas station. I think the radiator's cracked. Some guy there said he'd take a look at it."

The gas station is miles back. He must have hitchhiked. Ice fetters your wrist. You look down at his hand, and his lips close over yours from below, cold and trembling. How have you invented one so like yourself that it would warm itself by burrowing inside? You would kiss him again for the strangeness it stirs although common sense tells you he shouldn't be here uninvited. In your world, however, different rules have always applied.

"I was just heading out," you say, taking precaution. The knob on his face appears to turn, and a quick thrill shrieks inside you. Maybe he's scrutinizing your reaction. Maybe he can smell fear like a dog. He walks stiffly over to the stove where steam curls from a tea cup and stands over a burner to rub the cold from his hands. He's calling your bluff.

"Come on. I just got here," he says in a lightened tone. A nervous giggle works its way through your chest. You hate this about yourself, your tendency toward giddiness when you're scared. Like a damp machine malfunctioning, you sweat and your body crosses emotional wires. There could be a gun to your head and fear would bubble out in laughter. He likes that you're smiling. "I just drove miles for you," he adds as he swaggers toward you, and presses his mouth to yours again, staunch like a pinch affirming you're real. You see it in his face as he moves away; there is a beauty unused to itself. It is something you've uncovered, and sensing this somehow intrigues you. "I had to see you. To make you feel me again." His smile is bruised and hard and childlike, so that in it you remember everything, all the stories he's told. Like this, he's given you a function, an ability to turn someone human, to turn back into itself what the world has estranged though it sickens you now to remember.

"I need you to hold me down," he says, returning to the counter. He dunks your teabag. A giggle escapes. "You're different," he then accuses as if it accosts him. "Don't be scared. I only came to find out why." Again, softness, and it is this toying that repels you, for how it confuses and makes you unpoised.

"That's why you drove all the way here?"

He nods. What does he *mean hold me down*? His head drops, and he staggers backward a few paces. "Why are you afraid of me? You don't answer your phone." You can't, and he's reminding you why. "Look," he says then, holding out his arms full of fresh burns. It's what he'd been trying to show you at the door. "Just *like* me again."

"Victor, I can't..." You want to say *help you*.

"Yes, you can." His breath in your face is feral.

"No, I was wrong." Something in you is breaking, trying to get away. God, how truly dumb you are, Ror. The phone rings, and as you race toward it something cold slams against your throat. You're being dragged across the floor on your back. Breath lurches from you but can't find a way out, the ringing now muffled and far.

"We are fate," he says, his voice reverberating in his thin legs. You look up but cannot focus. This is not real. "I asked God for an angel, and there you were calling me back from the grave." The ringing stops. You're in his lap. "So sweetly," he whispers, searching your face for concession with a flat hand. There is the boy; you see it in him still, sitting on the surface like a mask. "I don't know what to do right now, Aurora." He's petting your face. What is that smell? "I don't know what to do. And I hurt you. God, I didn't mean to hurt you," he says, pummeling his forearm with his fist just above your head. The sound is sickening on the burns.

"Stop," you whisper, your voice hoarse. It feels like there's a bar against your throat or something tied; you can't swallow. You raise your hand to touch it then wearily sit up, half expecting to be struck down again.

"You said you wanted to hold me, to take the pain away. You were so good, Aurora. I knew you could. But now you're staring at me like some freak you don't want near you. Why don't you want to hold me? Why aren't you happy to see me?"

"You choked me, Victor. For God's sake."

"You shouldn't have said those things," he says peremptorily locking your gaze, you sitting before him, he stroking your head. "You said you'd help me." He strokes, and you're a dog beneath his hand, being pushed deeper and deeper into the floor.

"That's why you came here." You did this.

"You said you'd help me."

Your heart is not cold. It touches and is touched so that when something flies from it, it is paper. It is a boy whose wings have been clipped and bleeding so long that to listen to his song is not enough. To suture and to mend: these are your ways. And so the song is odd, and so it brings you close to it, and so you feel it bleating and hold yourself out, hold yourself out to the pulse and the rag, hold yourself out to the blow. For what is not clipped has begun to aberrate, to stray.

He looks at you defeated, with eyes that seem to be searching for some way out of the chaos. *Come closer.* Set a hand on his back; his shirt is warm with perspiration, warm with the scent of burning. Tentatively, believing love begets love, you slide a hand to his shoulder, pulling it gently toward you, pulling him in so close that you've become aware of your own breathing and are trying not to breathe at all.

Broken is a process, I say, breaking out of my narration.

Nor understands. "Continue. I'm not judging you. I can't say I'd do the same, but I'm not judging you." The angel's face is round like the moon.

"Sometime after this you realize the violence you've inflicted on yourself has an external counterpart that you've somehow drawn near. The bitterness of the wound is palatable. Your tongue swelling in your mouth, the metal blood, whether from your hands or his is in punishment. This punishment hadn't scared you until now."

His eyes are bright. His grimace snags your heart. You hear your cell phone ringing, and you start but make no effort to answer. "Your phone," he says with a grin. You understand this to mean you can answer it. Things are shaky when you try, and you have to concentrate to grab hold of the table and raise yourself to your feet.

Thwack. Your chin hits a chair.

Your mouth fills with blood.

"I can't help you like this," you say from the floor, hands shielding your face, the giggle in your voice disguising the fright; your blood a foam gag.

"Help me what?" he asks, thinking you're not taking this seriously. "You're trying to get away from me, Rora."

You raise a hand to your mouth, striking out your wrist with a red bar. He has you by the collar, fist hard against your neck. "They'll worry is all."

"Then maybe you should pick up next time," he says with a guffaw, letting go and nudging you playfully in the thigh. It rings again, and he bows and holds his hand out, welcoming you to take it. The laughter comes harder now, and tears stream from your eyes in fright. Dashing toward your phone on the counter, he's mocking you as he trips and falls. God, how you hate yourself, this hatred retarding your movement, so that it takes both hands on the door handle to heave it past the ice. Cotton slips around your toes as you stumble from the deck's edge in your socks and stagger into the yard. You hear his breathing behind you near the edge of the drive.

"You shouldn't have promised those things." A hand claps your shoulder. A quiet rasp escapes. He lays you out flat with his body and whispers unintelligibly in your ear.

The sky is black and still, erasing your breath in small clouds. "Victor?" you ask in desperation, tongue swelling in your mouth. His knuckles against your cheek bruising, he lifts you by the collar and then strangely sets you down.

You cannot imagine the wrongs done to this boy.

"You shouldn't have promised those things," he says again, distractedly, river reeds burning in the black eye, so that you notice he is no longer restraining you. In fact, he's backing off, and easing himself onto the ground so that scrambling on your knees away from him seems frightfully incongruous, easy and wrong.

A hand has pierced the landscape with its wet dark boughs. A hand has brushed the needle and stopped the night. In silence, as you scramble, everything around you has stopped. Black trees. White ground. Black sky. Black wing. White cloud.

I look at the angel in disbelief, my heart full of wind and erasure. *Nor, I can't breathe.* How?

The angel's eyes are closed, almost swollen beneath their lids.

But Victor has gotten to his feet, and by the time you reach the deck, he's kicked your shin into its base and shoved your face down. He's dragging you over the threshold of the open door. Your body is a thing that you carry. You will leave it here.

What has crawled out beneath victim knows no mercy. It has seen what one becomes and cannot accept this fate. The rooms spins and you stagger into him, no fight as the lower corner of your sweater fills with blood. You will remember it like the tearing of a sheet, slowly deliberately blood rushing into the opening, warmth emptying out as he swings you to your knees and you fall on your face in your humiliated body.

When you wake, you're gagging on his tongue, a taste like ash in your mouth, his hand searing into your neck, each finger a clamp he uses to hold you up to his vacant smile. He is inside you. The teeth behind his lips bruise as he presses your face to his then lets you fall back, your head whacking the floor, so the picture flickers and turns to black fear. Your body thumps the base of the couch in a rhythm in tune to your throbbing head. I am not here, you say within yourself. I am not here. I am not here. I am not here.

The body lies still. A log falls into ash. Tiny flakes drift by the window, and all is deathly still when he finally gets off.

A few days later his body will be found on the roadside, everything as planned.

GOODNESS.

"Dr. Rutch, do you believe we house our ancestors?"

"Please, explain."

"I wanted to believe I was good. Any time I did anything to assert myself and it hurt others, I dissociated with that part of me until I began to think I housed a demon that wanted me dead. My side wavered; I'd shift to the left and there the pathetic mute lay, a sack too stupid to get it right." He folds his hands into his lap while I slip out of my shoes. "What it leaves me with is the wonder, if I'm not in a way predisposed to recreating the victim as existed with my ancestry; if there is not a particular rhythm to the blood flowing through me that shudders when it falls against a wall. It has associated that shudder with love and everything in my life has directed me here." I pause, and the doctor nods slowly. "I've played the part well, trained myself to hold out for the kick and to make myself small. The first time I watched her slip into the box was such beauty, the snow fallen around the ruins of an old house. I stashed her there and swept the door closed never to return." Expecting judgment, I look up, but find only an amiable stare. "Despite her screams and the sound of rubbing on the horsehair walls, the trepid crawl across sand-strewn boards. The way knees can be mashed into paste. You've seen these parts of me and what they become. Everything was dead inside until I left. Then I realized it had only been precursor to what would come."

"So if I am to understand you correctly, there is a cycle

of abuse within your family that you too have fallen into. And you're having difficulty reconciling this with the idea of what you believe coming true for you?"

"Yes. I am then laden with unbearable guilt. It makes me responsible. I've allowed for patterns inherent in the family to take root. By wanting to know what it was like for my grandmother, by wanting to know how, I drew these things. Without taking an active role in my own happiness, I've accepted a victim's life. That I've done this, that my passivity caused this, I can't get past. How stupid I've been in love, how careless, how naïve."

"Aurora, I'm reminded of a drug addict I saw once, an artist like yourself but of the visual arts. In destroying himself, he destroyed his family and all that he loved. Recovery forces us to live responsibly, and one of the first steps is taking responsibility for what we've done. On looking back at the ruin in his wake, he, too, was laden with tremendous guilt. It weighed on his soul to the point that he tried within his first month here to hang himself.

"What I want to say is that you're not alone in this. 'God grant me the serenity to accept the things I cannot change, the courage to change the things I can and the wisdom to know the difference.' Sit with it for a while. See if it doesn't somehow offer something. The young man I spoke of found solace within this prayer and the strength to forgive himself. Recovery is a process and like all processes it takes time. The movement is not only forward, I might add.

"We aren't born into knowledge; these things aren't so overt. Let yourself be human."

93

PART 2.

Who, if I cried out, would hear me of the angels? And if, composed itself, one took me to its heart I would die in its presence. Because beauty is nothing more than a horrific beginning that we bear almost to breaking out of sheer awe of what would have us dead. Every angel is terrifying.

From **The First Duino Elegy**,
RAINER MARIA RILKE

THE ONE TO RELEASE ME hasn't returned. I hear the cranes at night: pods being torn from their throats clatter onto blank fields. Sleep, the frail wind. Still the crickets. Still the soft breath of the coyote on the screen. You want to know where I've been? I've kept a record of everything.

We aren't blameless at all for wanting love. They have sent someone: a boy knocking his head against the wall, a chair on two legs tipped into the bars. Human breath in the throat of the bird. I know those in darkness.

Here there is a new measurement: a machine pushing water against the crop.

You want the story? The story is fragmented, the story raw. It spans landscapes patched together by scenes. If I were to show you—there is the angel disinterring what I've made. He is not unkind. There is intention in his actions. He would save. But what saves is not always what you'd imagined. Maybe that's why it is dark for him. His heart is not cold. It touches and is touched so that when something flies from it, it is paper. It is a boy whose wings have been clipped and bleeding so long that to listen to his song is not enough. To suture and to mend: these are our ways. And so the song is odd, and so it brings me close to it, and so I feel it bleating and hold myself out, hold myself out to the pulse and the rag, hold myself out to the blow. What is not clipped has begun to aberrate, to stray.

How resilient the heart looks in this light; it is not as I thought. Come closer. How have I invented one so like myself he would warm that place by burrowing inside?

On the cusp, shades of pine. The moon has not found this night it being early and darkness having descended so certainly. And so it has gone from melancholy to gloom. The heart does not do in this bitter landscape.

If I could just fashion the hands to draw the girl out, if I could just fashion a room, or cradle her close enough, and if my hands were God's, wounded for there we are open, for there we are vulnerable… All these scars crying, be gentle with me. In affliction, they lay themselves before you.

"Do not be afraid of who you are in darkness," I hear, and so I reach in and find in me a place destroyed. The water has surged to great heights. My hands have removed the coffer, this yellow tie.

In my head the child bangs something out on the piano. Everything I know I have forgotten. I berate myself. I hate myself. What has happened? He got in. I got out. Why am I still here? Forgive me, but I have no one to tell. Do you know who I am? I've lost my way. I draw blood from my arm as I draw breath. From love perversion. Do not back away though my need is strong. Do not leave me to mythologize.

Out here the wind travels untethered, unbound. It leaps through the grass; it clatters through pine; it whorls its heavy masculine form, benign.
It is not that I don't believe, but that I've lived and compromised the self often enough to know sacrifice. Love does not ask this of us. What is this force, this being so like love in aspect and array? Love's shadow side?

The ceiling panels lift in succession. What has been drawn resides within this muscle stripped like fruit.
The man before me in the darkness. A sky of burnt umber. The wind is a hive.

Mind grinds to a halt so that the words slur at times and stop. What is the use? When all have rallied to the other side and the girl has not surfaced. I promised myself I would do this, but I want so little of this world. Where can I rest for a while? Release the pressure in my skull?

From the corner the cricket the cat had yesterday tries a mangled hymn, goes silent.

THE MARTYRED BIRD.

The angel has not opened his eyes. He doesn't understand what is asked of him. His tongue is a dry plug. The man cuffs him again. "Martyred bird." His boot nudges Nor's legs. Another man laughs. They are not men but pawns.

Nor spews a ribbon of phlegm and rests his head again in the pale dirt. The dryness in his mouth—is it sand he inhales?—bites at his nose like fleas and burns.

Discomfort draws him in and out of consciousness so that when he's later rolled to his back, he's shocked to find himself within a dim corridor. The man retracts a boot from his side and Nor follows his movement, the fluid pivot like the wave of a flag as two men lift him and press his contusions alive. Sand shakes over his dry lips. The voices go silent. A key ticks in a lock. Metal scrapes metal as a door is wound back on its pulley to reveal a dark steel-framed cell, at its center a cage.

OUTSIDE.

The sky, gray with light, portends horrific things. Its energy snaps at the nerves, demanding vigilance, so that I sleep with a stone in my palm as amulet. It holds the blue-gray clouds buoyant in the white pines, and the man at the edge of the field barely visible.

A tin box expands; there are dogs in the distance. I wake still not knowing how to do this. Through the diaphanous curtains, I know the sky unabashedly bare as I swipe my cell phone from the night stand and press it still. The heater ticks in the corner. The gray floor creaks beneath my blue-white feet. Why hadn't they kept me longer on the ward?

Winter sunlight slants into the village, where grasses and trees don morning hoar. My Honda sits in the shadow of a large oak tree covered in ice. I crack it open and squeeze into the back seat for the scraper as the door slams shut on my calf. Punishment. I pull it inside and turn the key, cold billowing out on my legs before I can switch off the fan. I lean my head on the wheel *get me through this get me through* but I don't want to be outside again.

Everything is frozen, my appendages red ice as I bump the scraper over the windshield and curse my ungloved hands.

In the accounting firm office with the burnt orange floor, I switch on the computer and settle back into my chair when I realize I can't do anything. In my head I'm gone, travelling through a place I once was, throwing off a life stated and dull. There is a grove at the roadside, trees bedecked in orange yield, and I am abandoned to the lush green grasses of citrus groves and wetland swamps.

Try to deny that you know this place. A voice coaxes.

I slam its mouth shut with the drawer of the file cabinet.

It rolls free again. *Do you think it was an accident that you surfaced here?*

Here is deep in the Florida backwoods where shacks litter the landscape like what within has been cast aside. Mammoth vines drape overhead like arms slung over the depressed bodies of trees, everything being shoved back down into earth all at once. What dare bare itself in these barren woods are only a couple of raptors ravaging the body of a wild cat in a ditch. Is it shame that drives them here? These two faces turned toward me in hunger, guardians hung on the gate of the otherworld, henchmen squatting at the roadside, their gray faces gathered around eyes from which can be read: you should not be here. I glance from the vultures to the shack in the distance when the hulking form of a man darkens my car.

I jerk back, upsetting the travel mug at the edge of my desk. Mani is hovering over my cubicle with a smirk on his face. The man hadn't been there.

"You mean to tell me they still haven't gotten you a splash guard for that thing?" he says, trying to catch the mug as it plunks down at his feet with a tinny sound.

"Actually, I think it's the splash guard that caused this damned mess in the first place," I respond nervously. I'm wrestling with the top drawer of my desk to catch some of the runoff on the scraps of poems and pens lying there. With a brown napkin found in its recesses, I swab the lip of the desk and tip the keyboard upside down so that a trickle of black tea spills out. Shit. He's amusedly watching me as I balance the keyboard on the edge of the chair to drain and rush to the break room for a roll of towel paper. Thankfully, the room is empty. When I return to my desk, however, Mani is still there, modeling a green and white checked

Abercrombie dress shirt, hands in the pockets of his khaki pants, dark hair swept back like plastic.

I flip the keyboard back onto the desk, my clumsiness apparent as the cord snags on the arm and I trip over the protruding foot of my swivel chair. Mani catches me as I flop backward. I want to cry.

"You got it under control now?" he asks as he rips off a few paper towels and mops up the remaining puddles before shutting the computer down. He squats down next to me and dabs at the floor.

"I think I'll manage."

"Welcome back," he says then, rising and knocking me gently on the arm. I feel my face flush. *God, I don't want to be here.* He watches me for a moment before adding, "Why don't you go help Janet downstairs, where they're back-logged in archives?"

Archives? Am I being demoted?

On Friday, I flush both bottles of pills, untouched since my release. "He hasn't come," I say to the cat with throaty heaviness after a week of pretending, feeling ridiculous in a fuchsia shift and striped arm warmers while the rest of the office strolled by in winter neutrals. It had been my attempt at rousing my morale. A moonstone dangles from a black cord at my throat. I pull the dress up over my head and fix myself a salad of cold salmon and pears, which I eat in my bra and panties while standing staring listlessly at the beat up carpet in the front room. My eyes shift to the white-washed wrought iron bed, the antiquated crystal chandelier, the chipped linoleum floor. My heart retracts; the brain unwilling to follow through even the most mundane movements. A bite of pear slips from my mouth back to plate, the message cancelled before the action is complete; the emotion too tired to carry me, the apathetic shove into the orifice. My hands want to die; my mouth... When I lift my hand to finish the poem I had begun earlier in the day, there is heaviness in me, the pen tearing at the notebook.

The molding is covered in dust I notice, pulling on a

wool trench coat and my green Hunters, and rushing through the stairwell to escape into the night. I slip down onto the ground against the house, the weather with its blustery gray head and tempestuous squalls reassuring me I haven't been abandoned. In the darkness of the duplex, gazing into the shadowed street, where snow drags across a bare patch of road, I whisper, *Nor, are you there?* He has always just been there, and I feel in that dumb empty that follows confession, I've lost him. Nor is gone.

"What is that?" Mani asks, gingerly running his hand over the back of my shoulder the next day.

I swivel the chair and elude him. "I fell asleep on a pen," I say dismissively, slipping my arms into the sleeves of my cardigan before he can get a better look. "I guess I won't be going sleeveless at the meeting," I add with a smile as if we've shared something I'm now taking back.

He looks distracted.

I get up and walk to the restroom where I meticulously reapply lipstick and then study the mirror for my faults. After re-parting my hair in the center and combing the long auburn strands flat around my face, I decide I need more eyeliner. More blush. Happy, happy blush. I freeze in the mirror, hands in my hair, when a consultant appears around the corner. I pull my cheeks back in an attempted smile. I wait until the stall door creaks and scuffs to a close before I venture to move again, to run my hands beneath the tap and flatten the strands into a side part again. I stick out my tongue at my reflection, bite my lips into plumping, slap my cheeks into further blushing, then hasten out of the room at the sound of the hard flush.

Later Mani tosses his business card on my desk, *I want to die, Mani* his private number scrolled across the back, before propping himself there as well. He leans in conspiratorially with his private-eye edge, his cocky do-or-dare. What does he want from me? I straighten up defensively when he begins unbuttoning his shirt sleeves, folding them as if tucking something away. The verdant green plaid brightens his eyes, and the creases along his mouth form provocative ridges when he smiles. His dark hair up close gleams almost white. Another of my saviors? He's sitting so close I can smell the gritty residue of sweat mixed with paste, deodorant warming beneath his arms.

Would it be all right if he held me?

"Aurora."

"Yeah." Along his arms stretch white scars of what has been leaked and left behind.

"Maybe you should start seeing that shrink again."

I look up as he sets a hand on my shoulder, and it begins to exude a strange heat. *We are the same we are the same we are the same we are the same* "It gets easier," he says as he rises, the fabric on my shoulder filling with cool, damp emptiness.

I force a smile on his departure, and there is the knife again stabbing at my heart; I'm doing it and cannot stop. I wipe my nose on the inside of my dress and dry my eyes on the cuffs of my sweater. What do I care? It is as if everything were in recession and I'm falling. Nothing grounds or sustains, so that there's nothing to hold onto. Where is Nor? Why am I alone?

When I get home, there is a boy on the stairs carving the letters of my name into his arm, curving the legs of each artfully, assiduously. He stays the night, sleeps in my bed though I don't want him there. I have never wanted him there. I lay out the goddess cards in a ring of protection, but he too is inside. Come to me, Nor, I cry, numb to everything now. Come to me, I supplicate, calling across the visions in fear. Why doesn't he come? Why is no one here?

CAPTIVE.

A metal table resides in the corner against the bars. Nor drags it through the pile of feathers he's gathered as his bed, its hollow legs screeching across the floor. He stops at the center and climbs atop to the parallel bars that form the ceiling of his cage. Slowly and methodically, he swings down one side then up the other, trying to rid himself of his angst, trying to block out the monologues playing out within, the dialogues, as if he could speak.

The jangle of keys against the outer door prompts his dismount, and he falls into the chair in the far corner, tipping it into the wall. Something slides a ceramic plate beneath the bars. Chicken, again. His keeper mocks him.

What is he doing here?

BIRD. Tonight my skin splinters and I know the light won't leave me. When it does, I am what he has made: the kindled wood, the ash lay bare under his father's wedge. All of this passes through the body. And so you will not speak, so you will not find the boy, he feeds his hands through the orifice that stills your heart. Feeds your body like prey, splays like a bird conveying wisdom.

The bird is nothing here; just vehicle, just skin. The bird is ignorance; the bird what the demiurge asks it to become. Leviathan. What in him peals in laughter I have solicited from the basest self. We are what we draw toward us. I cannot but claim this.

HOLLOW INSTRUMENT.

Winter is a field littered with the wings of white swans. The heart is cold. Love stagnates. I cannot drag myself from bed. When the alarm sounds again, I hurl the phone into the wall where it nicks the plaster before falling apart. This is followed by a fist to the headboard, an egg inflating on my middle knuckle as if the effects were cumulative.

When I roll to the bed's edge and plunge to the floor, punishing myself further, it further frightens Rogue, my cat, who takes shelter beneath the base of a plant at the apartment's far end. Here I will remain with my arm crunched beneath my hip bone, discipline intact. I will not shift though it eventually goes numb. I'll lie catatonic until the cat returns and drapes her belly over my head.

Then, eventually, the prospect of being unemployed and homeless less appealing than the alternative, I'll drag myself to my feet and open a bureau drawer, haul a pair of black trousers and a scoop neck eggplant top from their disheveled piles, and throw them on. I'll quickly tie up my hair, brush my teeth, and then head into the kitchen to feed the cat.

Why can't I be sick? Why can't I be crazy for another day?

Rogue weaves through my legs and slams her head against the lower cupboards at the clip of the tin key. There is the child from the crone's office again dying on the rug. Thump, thump. When I bend down with the saucer to place it on Rogue's mat, she nudges my hand and spills the juices before burrowing her maw into the dish. The pink child is still there as Rogue catches a piece of flesh on her lip. How she bobs her head and stretches her tongue as I lower myself to the floor, hoping to close the lid to the hollowness. Hot tears pool in my eyes and run onto the hand curled under my face. A hard gasp and Rogue lifts her head toward me, the cloudy veil not fully receded from her eyes. *A sleeve of skin, the loose dark socket bristled with fur. I'm looking out the eyes, the animal ascending.*

Half-heartedly, I rise and rinse out the tin, letting the water scald my hands. I bundle up and gather the pieces of my cell phone into a pocket before swiping a shovel from a darkened corner of the upper landing and trudging the rest of the way down the stairs.

There is safety in a sky so opaque and close: a shade fashioned to the bulb when we can't bear its starkness, and in the freshly fallen snow, I brighten just a bit. *As you've asked for me, I've sent for you.* I'm reflecting on the conversation while heaving shovelfuls of snow higher and harder than necessary into the lawn beside my car when a dragging sound takes me out of my thoughts.

My neighbor, Ms. Brisby, stuffed in a magenta parka and colorful knit cap, is trailing her red plastic shovel over the freshly plowed street in my direction. Not that I particularly like the middle-aged busybody, but because I'm making a case for unpunctuality, I ignore my throbbing knuckles and the ache in my arm, tighten my grip on the handle, and begin chipping snow from the base of the woman's white Escalade parked in front of my car.

"Your brother was here feeding the cat for a few weeks. Everything all right?" she asks, curling her rainbow mittens over her shovel as I continue to liberate the giant white beast. Her teeth are the color of yellow snow.

"Would you believe I stabbed myself and ended up on a psych ward? They don't know yet if I just didn't want to live, or what."

Ms. Brisby stares uneasily off down the street. I stop then

in mid-thrust and smile, a frisson against the clopping heart.

"Oh, you're pulling my leg!" the woman expels with a snort.

"Yes, everything's fine, Ms. Brisby." I've finished digging her out and am reaching into the side panel of the door for a blue-bristled snow brush. I use this to sweep the rest of the car clean while the woman scrutinizes the neighborhood before climbing in. It doesn't matter what I say to her. This isn't real.

Once Ms. Brisby's out of sight, I drop the shovel at the apartment entrance and break into a run across snow-covered lawns. The winter sky is browning at the horizon, and clouds are being cleared off in shrieks that come from the school ground. Blue peers in from the top, and I race harder against its threat of exposure as I veer into the park and drift to my knees in a pile of snow. At the edge of the pond beside the path, a blond duck's wing pulses a quarter note in sleep. The one beside her does not nudge her awake, does not ask her to silence what she cannot control. My breath is erratic and shallow. I attempt to draw it in, to ascertain its ragged form from the wind before rising again and trudging the last few steps toward the swings.

There I shake the chains to dislodge the snow before settling on a black rubber strip. I used to have an angel named Nor, I think, backing up and letting go, pulling against the dark links and folding my legs in propulsion until I'm a pendulum swinging on a chain, soaring back and forth through an empty park, a cold white star claimed by winter and held on its thread. Vertigo drifts in. The arc widens and recedes.

I imagine my breath drifting out across floorboards; the house frozen beneath my cheek, my slate hands strewn with sand. I'm leaning back. I'm losing myself in the motion, recalling myself in the cage, where there is strangely comfort and safety to be found. But the sky has begun to warm and when I tilt my head back a second time, it is into beige-tinged clouds and the damp ache of winter giving up.

Come back you white beast, reclaim your demesne, take me under and beneath a frozen mound.

Still I am strung to this swing, rocking the neglectful sky, inadvertently churning what will become a world I despise, what will melt and abandon and become plastic and steel and tar.

A tug at the reins forces me higher until there's a jerk at the top of each swoop jaunting the swing. Again and again how the world is jarred and how hatefully I pump into brightening the hateful sky as though it were my intention. From a pinnacle of arc, I spring and come down. There is chaos in my head, chaos in the rumble of plows in the distance, chaos in metal being dragged, a whistled reverse, a squealing belt, voices raised into what longs to mute until I'm thoroughly wet and numb, lying there on the ground.

It was safe in the House of Winter. I clap my boots together then, sweeping through snow and ice and flapping my arms. It feels ironic, however, carving an angel, so that when the snow that gathers between my legs is smoothed into a clean skirt and the wings have unfurled fully beneath my arms, I carefully sit up, and shifting my weight onto my hip, carve the word 'asshole' into its breast. Then slowly and consciously I raise myself to my feet and walk off.

How easily air severs the bonds between things, the blue sky always in recession.

Later when I peel away the black trousers and thong, my skin is numb and red. I put my hands to my ass cheeks and feel the thick slate slabs. When I speak to Rogue I lisp, my *th*ongue den*th*e with cold. She prances toward me, belly swaying while she trills in delight. I pick her up and press her to my chest, smiling bitter sweetly as I realize what I've done. But I don't care. There's sand in my heart.

The straw-like strands of frozen hair quickly thaw and dampen the pillow after I've drawn the curtains and climbed naked and red back into bed. I'll convince myself I'm sick if I have to. Hell, I want to die. Isn't that sickness? The soft sheets are no consolation, nor the cat that climbs onto my chest as I pull the blanket up. When I free my hands to scratch her ears it's in aggression, and when she bites me it feels deserved.

There is a brown paper bag of glass in the drawer where I've collected it, the one within already tempered at the thought. I will get a towel from the bath and empty the contents onto the carpet. I will crush it into shards until blood flows from my hands in catharsis, and things move out of me and beyond. Then I'll curl up with the towel wrapped around my hands and cry myself to sleep.

When I wake the ceiling is draped in golden webs. A colossal arachnid stitches the world with luminous thread, and I blink to clear the dream field which lingers. Divinity. I am not alone, I think, when all at once the light recedes and winter's blues diffuse from the curtains' edges. What do you want from me?

THE BODY SHARED. Now that we share the body what has come before is only prelude. And they are like plums swollen and taut, fists caught in my arms, trapped there. It is only that I ache that I do not return your embrace. And the body is a bag that I set inside the room, its legs kicked out beneath it, the thwack of the skull against the bed board, and me sitting stunned inside the sound.

THE BODY SHARED.

The world has changed its face again. Low clouds have come in warning, the black bird roosting on the sill, the one that cast a shadow over the window. Something I did woke him. All is not without repercussion, he seemed to be saying as he shuffled his feet and the periphery wavered and light changed form.

My car lies half a block in the distance. The streets are filling with freezing rain, which drags at my pant legs like a needy child as I fumble with the keys in my hand. For heavily and slowly, with the rain that falls, come the savagery of voices and the figure of a man. In my head, he is stalking me. He pulls me to the ground, holding me there by the strands of hair trapping me under his boot sole. Reach out for an end and be taken slowly into his world, bound to him in contempt. A black smear grows through the chest cavity. I know this as it works repulsively through. There is flatness here, what scrapes the ocean floor and sands us clean.

What is this place so dark in me that darkness consoles?

Why do you want to know this? a voice returns, knowing what such questions bring.

Because it is mine like flight is yours. Because it came to me for me to explore.

I am in the car, setting the locks. His face is at the window, beastly in the rain, long tresses dividing its features into parts, my body a shiver of nerves. What is it the victim tries to kill? The one within who let this happen, the one with

115

lidless eyes.

Open up, Aurora.

It wants me to see so that it can punish. It has drawn me because it knows I know how. Sheets of rain pummel the car. I feel the tires lift, floating as the world floods, and I am relinquished to its whim.

His body falls across the door. Oh, Aurora it's only Nor.

"Nor, you dark bird. Get in."

"What was that?"

Nor feels like a squirrel knocked dumb, dropped to the pavement and spinning on the walk. Black stars scatter at his frontal lobes. Has he been dropped? Pushed from a bough? The mist adds to his vertigo. The black stars churn.

HOW COULD.

His wings are filling the car. There is a snapping sound and then stillness, the smell of rain in flood. I'm wiping steam from the window with the cuff of my sleeve, compulsively moving my hand around, into the metal frame and around. I want to be distracted; I want to feel love. He searches my face for admission before finding my lips with his hand.

Doesn't he remember? What should he remember? He's touching me, his frame so large it fills the cab, wings askew and bent, one jammed against the door, another poking the fabric overhead, the car matting and twisting the pinioned things as I hold on.

How could God be so cruel as to send such a thing? With a foreign voice and a face tilted toward mine, the vision clears for a moment. I wake in a haze, raise a hand to the dark head of hair, grasping a handful to steady myself there.

"Whatever you fear has already happened," he says.

GOD.

Whatever I fear. Whatever I fear. He is at the bottom of the pen.
When his hands leave me how can I live?

> *If that god weren't real!*
> What god?
> *Aurora, are you in my head?*
> What god?

It is late when we make our way up the apartment stairs.
Why does it feel like falling into him would save me? And
what is with his wings? Tacked together like a nuisance of
hair that falls in the face, a blasphemous display. I touch my
mouth, bite at my bottom lip in reflection, remembering the
feel of parchment, the salt and the paste, my rain-darkened
hair, the dark mark across my cheek, my pale eyes. My tank
top is dampened across the middle and the curve of my hip
peaks from the low cut sable cords as he lowers me into his
lap on a kitchen chair. A sip of beer spills unevenly across
my lips. *Make me feel other than this darkness inside.* I swallow.
The damn grapes. Prometheus. All whom the gods use. *We
begin again in chaos*, he says, touching my hand to his heart.
There is nothing inside. What does God want from me?

He wants to know if we can outgrow him. His look is penetrat-
ing, as if he assumes I have the capacity to comprehend.

Outgrow God? I pull away.

"Like a parent or authority figure," he says aloud, letting
me up. I ease into a chair across from him and proceed to

tug at the wet fabric on my calves. "Instead of seeking the answers for yourself, you're always dragging God into it, trying to ascertain his intentions."

"They're one in the same. God created my heart." Silence. He closes his eyes and inhales. When he opens them again, they're white like a bird's. Where has he come from? "How can you outgrow the creator? Your conception of God would have to be wrong."

That's just it.

Why is he saying this? Confusing me like this? I can't even support myself or hold a job. I run a weft of hair through my lips, feeling the silky slide of single strands across my teeth. Although I haven't done this since I was a child, I suck at the silken cord and then strain it through my teeth, remembering the sweetness of balsam in the chestnut-colored locks. Does he find my behavior callow?

"Consider," he says in a voice hard and unamused. "You're always searching for approval, for validation from God. Are you there, God?" He is punchy in the gray light that fills the kitchen from a single bulb. "Is it really so bad that I pocketed the change from Dad's dresser, God? That I ate the girl's Cracker Jack's? That I followed him home?" I glance up to see that he knows. "Am I a bad person for wanting him dead, God? For filling the gas tank? Surveying the grounds?" Our eyes are locked on each other. "I wanted him to burn, God. What should I do now, God? Are you there, God?"

Stop! My eyes steam, and my cheeks flush hot.

Still he continues, "What if we outgrew that concept and became the one in charge? What if God were pushing us toward greater independence?"

I am silent for a very long time, embarrassed that I hadn't realized how much he knew.

The more Nor thinks about it, the more likely it seems. It would certainly explain his resistance; this battle that rages against the dastardly good. If he's wrong, well, it's the bad

119

seed to whom the parent responds with greater affection. But there he goes again with 'God the father'.

DEAD-END.

When I get up to fetch dry clothes from the bedroom, he remains hunched over his lap, hands clasped together, head down, so that I'm surprised when an arm extends in my path. I take his hand from my lower thigh, noticing at once the coating of down, the palest covering of webbed thing as I hold it before me. Oh Nor, your arms are sinewy animals, birds in their own right, rain-drenched things, yellowed where the fibers are dampened and clumped. I feel his eyes on me as he tilts his head, the glint of flame in some dank dark depth. Look away, Aurora. You have nothing left for this.

"Have you outgrown God, Nor?" I still haven't left the kitchen. Why do I want to cry?

"Haven't you?"

Damn it, where has he been?

I'm not sure that I know that answer, again he responds to my thought. He gives an unabashed smile when his chin, which is sliced, starts to bleed. Bronze strands coil in the dark mass, drying to frame his gaunt face. He approaches me again, uninhibited, heavy muscles soft like birds.

"Why are you doing this?" I ask, backing up. It's not fair that he takes so much.

"It's not cruelty but love." He pauses, and in that pause I know he's not considering me but his argument. "We are indivisible from God. God lives through us. God experiences human through us, which would mean we have to evolve God." he says finally as if the epiphany has just occurred to

121

him. *The same devoted flock of sheep would defy the evolutionary flow. Unchallenged, torpid…*

"You mean the concept of god, but not God. You keep applying the fatherly concept, the judgemental, controlling, punishing force. That god is dead because it cannot grow."

"What is God then?" he challenges, getting up.

"Why are you acting so naïve?"

"Not naïve. Elementary." Nor rubs at his forehead impatiently. "We've missed something," the angel continues. "I'm merely trying to recover it, so I'm going backwards. You were Catholic, a child fasting at age 5 because she'd thought she'd done something wrong, because she thought she could never be good enough… Maybe you'd sensed it then, how inadequate 'girl'…"

"We find ourselves the longer we live, you said before," I attempt, not wanting to hear what more he knows about me. "Isn't it the same with God?"

Nor is facing the window at the front of the apartment, blind drawn, velvet drape shut.

"Nor?" I say tentatively. He's scaring me.

"We find ourselves and God finds himself," he paraphrases thoughtlessly, his massive wings folded high on his back, stiff and cumbersome. *How to get sheep to think on their own and reject such puny measurements as wicked and good.*

I release a quiet laugh. "That's not what I was saying. If the larger we grow, the greater our capacity to know God…" But my voice trails off, for Nor's wings are ticking against each other, tearing against the metal bracket seemingly in repulsion. A crackling resounds like the snapping of chicken bones.

"Exactly, the range of your experience thus evolves God." Nor replies emphatically, as if I've proven the point he has been trying to make all along.

There is that same dead-end mirrored in her features. She's not pushing the ideas hard or far enough. *Do not enter* *her,* something internal warns. But how else convey this so that she catches on? Before Nor can examine his own motivations, however, before he can delve into the source of his building rage, how perfectly Aurora takes up the victim's role, the arachnid delving inward at his touch, and how perfectly springs his repulsion for the legless thing.

FALLEN LEAVES AND WANING WINTER LIGHT.

The stairwell darkens; the world closes in. A cold rush of air breaks out over my shoulders and neck as I fold my arms over my chest and sprint across the yard. Who is this shadow of an angel? Something in me knows. Something in me recognizes what it has drawn. Inner creates outer. I've harbored these fears on my own.

Fallen leaves and waning winter light draw to the periphery. Just as I sense the last of the sunlight when I finally stop, just as its warmth penetrates as I breach the trees, I will sense someone watching, not a stranger or man, but an entity that knows me intimately, a presence looking on. I have stolen to the edge of the Wisconsin River and as I step out of the woods and onto the matted grasses of its banks, everything empties. The brown river taking everything, strips the scene to remote, drab colors, despondency, hollowness, angst so that when Nor finally catches up, I cannot stand it anymore on the inside. I throw myself into his arms when a dark wing knocks me to the ground.

Is this in punishment, Nor wonders, stretching his wings awkwardly high. They are like arched sieves. What sort of trick? They stroke the air but do not fly; it's mockery, the inefficacy of the apparatus. He is so distracted, so caught up in himself that he doesn't notice the girl running toward him or the fright in her eyes as she's struck to the ground. A

124

blackbird caws in the distance. Another flies into the trees above.

"Shall I let you come in and move me? And in which way can I protest when it is not in the way I would have moved myself?" He looks up asking the bird, Aurora, God. He doesn't know any more than that he's been sent. But by what? That dark thing within drawing him to its side? The commanding beauty of its strength, its absolute power. Hasn't he somehow, in some way asked for this? And isn't it within his own command to commune with it, with what swells his limbs and surges through his core? Is it courage or cowardice that he would appeal to one who had the force he could not find within him otherwise? The thought is dizzying.

The bird chips at something, which it then rocks back and forth with a tap. Nor raises his head and scans the sky before stumbling his way back to the house, the slap of his wings against his thighs resounding as he beats them into cooperation in the frigid surround.

COME FORWARD.

Have I stopped breathing or is it displacement? Something observes in moments like these, so that what erupts in me is shame, shame to which I concede in a whimper, curling into myself in the leave-bedecked sand. There is nowhere to move on to, no safe place in this world. I lie there staring at the darkening trees while fear creeps in and cold. Was it benign? What was it that watched with the eyes of the conscious? What was it that made me feel shame? Was it God? I wanted to know, but Nor could not answer.

Far off in the distance coyotes yip and keen, hastening my trek back home. But I am hollow when I think of my angel and this drags in me even as I run.

A fevered hand dampens the ink and the letters swell as I raise a hand to my throat and swallow against the pain. It has already happened in the world within. *Whatever you fear has already happened.*

And so cruelty reveals itself, and the house changes form: the ones bringing love to the walls wield instead trauma on wavering knives and on the ends of shoes on glass rods and in blood that seeps into mortar. I cannot pretend I do not know these things. One does not go backward from knowledge. *Come forward then*, a voice beckons.

THE ONLY BRIGHT THING. *The only bright thing in the room shines with madness. Reckless as if the body were machine and he stripping the gears halting and chugging and spurting along. His animal maleness draws me. It is the arm he slings into my head as he reaches for me in the night, unaware of brutality, knowing only his own needs. And so it begins with a man so foreign from me that I mistake him for love. He seems to have come for me. In fact, he says he has, as if he's divined this somehow. He recognizes me for my beauty and I him for his. I have drawn him toward me from a dream and like this he seems a magician and we speak to each other from beyond.*

Until one day I witness something that makes the heart buck. It throws him from my arena and makes me question sacred. But he has answers and his love will not release me. It will have me though it becomes more and more apparent as I cling to the sensual just how difficult this holding on is going to be.

THE REPRESSED ONES.

When the tyrant finally reclaims her hold, it is deep in the night. The tick, tick, ticking of her lower eyelid marks her pace across the concrete floor. She stops abruptly, sensing the angel, his look forlorn as she unlocks the door, and henchmen flow from the outer reaches into sight. How innocent the pale skin against the drab darkness of uniform as they carry him.

"Jesus, Nor."

Then he is abandoned to a corridor of cells. There a girl whimpers, and he turns to face her.

"Aurora?" Nor questions, peering into the cage.

How she tears at her hair and snaps at the bars; how she beats her thighs and saws her wrists against the lock, for here is the one who took the reins from her mother's hands, and who in defiance fled; she, who strapped on experience like punishment, who took the world into her bed like a rabid monkey, and gave the attendant of all-that-wasn't-allowed free rein. Here is the caged one, abandoned, sex raw and gaping, huddling in a corner next to a blue plastic cot. And they are all there now, the repressed ones, in this room where the white gown shivers overhead.

"Christ, who taught you this child?" A stern one cloaked in habit rises from the crowd of children.

"I wanted to be good," another one cries while tucking her nimble fingers into her mouth. A yard opens out into a fenced pond beside a convent nursery. "The ducks are waiting to be fed. Old bread. It was in punishment they

128

said."

This is how she learned to treat the child, the child who didn't know what was good for her.

"How God swayed from the tire swing I'd made," an older girl with a bandaged knee goes on. "How he swayed back and forth in the light that filtered through the branches of the wagging bough. How he took the pale form of doll, a flaccid thing, how the light came as from the horizon, an aureole illuminating the prophet as it swung, a dead thing offering nothing."

"So that we never knew love," another child picks up the narrative thread. Nor turns to face her—but where is he?—the petticoat of her dress marked with mud where she'd knelt at the pond side and tipped bread into a bucket. "What it would really feel like when it touched our skin."

"Mary was a virgin," a whisper explains, a pale towheaded, cherubic thing.

Another continues. "And then he touched me, and made it hurt so I could lie there inculpably."

In vertigo, the angel spins around.

"When they came for her, she was only a carcass of a thing, and we all left the body then."

"But me and me and me," says the whispering one.

"And the boy pulling the legs out of the daddy longlegs so that it humps and humps and humps, this tiny button of a thing."

THE GRIEF GOD.

"Nor, where are you?" I cry in a fever from the surface, for the grief god has me and is slipping his hands down my throat, the god in white robes, the white-gloved god in a body that shuts itself down.

Within, plant leaves fall away from kern, slink down the length of body, and I'm falling at the god's knees, his fingers in my mouth, the warm broad forms weighing on my tongue, a scent so human slipping down the throat, a scent of parsnip and leek. His thumb rests on my bottom lip. His fumbling fingers prod and pry, bruising tenderly the space below my tongue.

The god's pleasure rests in process, seducing the body in touch. Sleep, he wills, his hands steeped now in confection. Sucking the stupor from his skin and yawning in ecstasy, my mouth clamps down. I grab hold of his robes to steady myself, and a soporific gust curls into my nostrils. I doze against it, nod, and shake my head free.

"What wishes to have you will wait," he whispers, and his breath is a wave of sleep knocking me firmly under a bed.

Nor, where are you?
But he cannot respond.
Nor, what have you seen? Why have you run?
Run? Yes, run. I destroy you in the end.

A voice and a face tilted toward mine. I wake and raise a hand to the dark head of hair, grasping a handful to steady myself there. It is the same moment. I am dragged here again.

What have I neglected to imagine? What have I neglected to see? The pain of absence strains the body to the point of lyricism, and I am a child left to ruminate alone.

Father, Father, the loon has gotten out. The ring has gone foul around the moon.

Nor stirs in his cage at her entrance while the man on the blue mat pales. I see the child in me soften too quickly, the man grabbing at her hair, the child at his feet, climbing assiduously as the dark floor crawls. God, how many times? How the mind curls, how it turns away in parts, how it hacks at the body to be free. She could have gnawed at the arms of her arms of her arms, this winter child watching from within, knowing violation from a place with no efficacy.

A scream reverberates: a cicada beneath the city grates.

The cells rattle in succession, and the children are covered in shame.

131

STRIPPED.

Voices on the cusp, the smell of ash and rust. I open my eyes and a heavy metal door hinges wide in my path. Curled in a ball one can see lean musculature made defective by a blackened emaciated limb. A cage rises around him at the center of the room and a stench that is not human as much as he is not. The uprooted divine, he lifts his head and lets it fall.

Plucked bird. Utter despondency shutting out and down. I reach out and it lives, the fingers curling over mine brightening now in fleshy hue.

Nor?

"We are dark sometimes. Sometimes we destroy. You are not there yet, Aurora. You can't know why. It is not as easy as this. There are things we're not seeing."

Dragging him through the corridors, I falter and regrip, his sinewy form slipping from my arms, his boney wings jutting into hip and thigh as I go. It's the bird on the strand I couldn't save. He's so broken. When he lifts his head the dark-ringed eyes set in sallow cheeks draw rage in me intermittent with sadness.

"Oh Aurora if you only knew how many it took to draw you, to hold your face toward the light that you might catch a glimpse."

"What shall I do now, Nor? What are you telling me?"

"Don't ask for this. Do not ask." Nor pleads. "To know the darkness, to know why some are punished, do not ask. Whatever you focus on becomes your fate," he warns, but what he means by this confounds. "Your obsession with the darkness breeds it until that darkness consumes and destroys."

He has seen things within me. He knows me better now. My head begins to fall before I meet his eyes. Is it this that loves so hard it could destroy itself in relinquishment?

"Ror, how is that love? These self-sacrificing, self-mutilating tendencies. The idea of punishment that comes from judgment and sin. The idea that we must suffer to be good, that it somehow makes us holy, somehow makes us divine."

"Some harbor more darkness than others," I say. I am one of Jung's suicides; one of those for whom escape becomes a coping mechanism; a way of life; one forever doomed to plunge from heights, to end the self if only to begin again.

"Oh Aurora."

I know now the one I become within. I know her rhetoric suave and chill. I know how she sabotages. How lazy and perilous, she leads me into a day, until another day slips by. And another. For she knows how the cat will suffer without pills and how easy it will be to hate myself with unwashed skin and teeth un-brushed, and the cat I've neglected dragging lethargically along at my side.

AWARENESS.

This is not a love story. The mellifluous ride through a chord that takes us into and back from love is struck quick here. At its end silence, lack, and the self, scrounging at the floor to gather what she can into her arms like some sort of beggar or miscreant. It is this self that is boxed in the cab of the truck and shipped off.

"I fell in love with an illusion and now that illusion is breaking me," I reveal, my chest heaving from the weight of the secret as it's released.

"So now it is time," the crone breathes, her contralto voice rich with melody as she turns into the room. Her hair is smooth now, cropped sleek and white. A pendulum hangs below her bust line from a black satin cord. It swings there as she leans against an armchair and motions for me to take a seat at the hearth.

"There is no savior," I announce, withdrawing a notebook from the leather satchel at my side.

"If mental anguish were a wound, a raw opening and you were to sit before it prying, these are the visions that would come." The crone closes the book and touching her face as if to suppress something there rests a hand over its green spine. "There is a portal that comes not from chanting or prayer, but from the body of one torn in despair. Leaves spill in messages. The one breached by the gods offers their knowledge…" When I raise my head it startles her.

"Your attention is on darkness, what brings the dark

things," the crone continues. "Your desire to know it gives it passage into the world. You are portal through which it seeks to live, so that your writing has the power of a living darkness that you've conjured and contained. Its darkness lives."

Am I Sybil? Pandora? What if it were true? What if one's existence contained that story? I imagine my body a vessel or jar releasing dark wrath on the world. What if we unwittingly became these things, what if just one spot of darkness and the curious urge in us to discover what it was caused it to expand and then not only expand but escape into the world through our own body and mind? So that essentially we were a Pandora's jar as well what fashioned it and unclasped its lid.

How beautiful the darkness when what within is bathed in pain, when it wears a voice that feels centuries long, a yowl, a timbre, everything struck and holding to nothing but the emptiness inside. A cry existing in time once, beyond it goes, it goes on, for we carry within us the place of its birthing. In the pain of the cry it is dark.

I am a child, a girl sitting on the floor in truffle-colored leggings and a pale sweater, slipping its hands in and out of the cuffs of its sleeves. *Whatever you focus on becomes your fate*, I hear in Nor's voice. That everything opens into something and then into its simplest rendering in the history of the world, we have our archetypes. But what when one explodes into something so complex that the mind cannot hold it stable long enough to describe it in linear terms? What when one becomes something greater than itself?

I slink to the floor, a dumb, dumb girl unable to ascertain anything beyond, for darkness is other things: a child that you terminate for instance and the man to whom you're a toy.

Do not ask for this. Is this what he meant? I'm dizzy with thought. This thing within driving me on, the impetus that does not long but to release into more of what it is.

135

THE OCEAN'S DEAD.

I lie beneath the wrought iron braces of the sewing table where I've contorted myself. When I lift a clammy hand to the cold, black bar and breach its frame with my head, the long unkempt tresses swaying before me, thoughts scattered, I cannot fathom what the white witch before me asks. I whisk them aside. What base thing thought itself divine?

"Tell me about the bird," the crone asks again. She is standing above me in white light.

It is on the last page of the diary, the diary his hands had touched, the diary that heard the shouts from the shower walls, and the tremor that fell over me like water that day he sent me cowering deep in the closet, clenching the towel to my dripping form. There the bird lies in thin water, dragged across the sand. There it sails its broken kite, its flight arrested, white wings tipped black, the slivered beak lain upon its back. There it drifts, the ocean's dead. What it signifies on those pages is concession. A girl relinquishing her claim to savior, relinquishing control. The earth is dying and she cannot save herself.

"Aurora, you were meant for this," the crone encourages.

"But I've failed." My hands slip from the bars and I tumble out onto the open floor.

"You cannot fail."

"Why then has the world stepped away? The interactions are surreal, as if I do not exist at all. Nothing is returned, and now what I love is darkening. Maybe Dr. Rutch was right."

"Do not belie your heart," the crone warns. "Proceed in love and you will not be broken. You have every right to ask for what is yours."

"Why did you leave me?" I ask after a time.

"Aurora, it was you who left me. You stopped listening within. Emotion is a powerful seductress but its powers are consumptive unless combined. Imagine yourself a shape-shifter. If you give completely to this thing, self is obliterated. What you must learn is to take all of who you are with you. Do not abandon; do not cast parts of yourself aside; do not give yourself to turmoil so that you don't have to decide; so that you are in the end inculpable. Use the wisdom that comes from within you. All of these characters are exaggerated extensions of self. We are the manifestations without us."

"What of the darkness that comes from within?" I still want to know.

Silver light spills like filament over the space the crone inhabits in the room. Her silver hair glistens like webs in hoarfrost, shimmering before their passage beneath the sun's thaw. Where sun cannot pass, the hearty stem anchors itself to the earth, a black bough in drift ever cast in winter hue.

"It is only that landscapes differ with perception," she explains. "If you were to walk your core what would you see?"

"A terrain divided into which a girl is tossed." And here I'm echoing Nor's plight, for here again is the girl in winter's cage. "At times an abyss with free-standing crags of black granite. A low fog snakes its way through the darkness illuminated by cold light. My heart is a black granite crag. There is no mercy in this place."

"Continue on."

DISINTERRED.

"What are you looking for?" Nor questions. I'm straddling a pit of sand, bowing over it, my hands cupping and spraying recklessly like a dog. "Ror, stop."

He takes my wrist and pushes the damp strands back from my face. The insolent things fall forward again, dragging sand across my nose and cheek and casting sparks of light across my vision as I stare at him as if I had not stopped moving, as if I could not catch up with myself. What can I say? How can I explain that what I search for is in vain? That my entire battle with this damned disease has yielded nothing? That I am a fool. I wrench my hand free from his and tip my head again down. I will dig. It busies me.

Nor gazes out onto a still sea. From time to time, I look up at him observing me, witnessing my frustration as fingertips scrape across coarse, dark stones and sand embeds itself beneath the nails. I relocate and begin again to disinter, my feet slipping deeper as I steady myself and plow the surface away, dispersing it easily. The lower I get the darker the sand, and the heavier and coarser it feels until I am on straddled knees one hand anchoring me head down in the pit. I scrape open the bottom and widen the lower walls, and the sand breathes a vacant, ragged dampness into my shoulders and heart, for what I disembowel leaks into core. My fingers sting as they scrape at stone. How cold and numb they feel, and how quickly the moon changes its face within the cloud when I retreat on my hands up the walls and reemerge.

Why am I doing this? I question, falling back defeated onto a mound of sand, my plaid shirt falling open to expose a white bikini and a skirt tied from a hooded sweatshirt: beauty, arched and stranded, chest heaving and sinking in the quarter moonlight. The angel is beside me.

"Why don't you do something?" I ask after a time, combatively rolling to my stomach at his feet.

"Shall I help you dig?" He is beginning to look more like a man, his wings less noticeable, dull shaggy hair.

"You torment me."

Nor yanks me then from the mound, drags me over shells into his lap until I'm covered in salt and sweat, and my hair, coarse from the sea, smells like its weeds. His eyes are illuminated with borrowed light. When his mouth comes down, I feel he could drain me. His hands are in my hair, matting it, touching my flushed skin, that swell of muscle along the inner thigh strung so that it opens my mouth. Over the strand the sea puddles out and I am the white light hung on him.

"I want to show you something," he says then, releasing me.

In his absence, blankness and the feeling I can't stand. I am alone with my graves and still water. Unable to follow.

I brush sand and shattered shells from my arms before noticing how the sting prolongs the reach of love, how in the abrasion he's somehow still on me, in me, touching me, and my skin, flecked with mica, is growing raw.

What would he show me?

There is a strange division; my body knocked backward as the space before me fills with the bodies of animals, a pack of feral dogs. One passes directly before me, its mouth torn in fight, a gaping hole over its terrible teeth. I lower myself to the ground as they pace like weightless coyotes and then burrow into the sand in succession. Where am I?

"Within." I look at him, nonplus, though this might explain how he knows so much. "What you've unearthed you've forced me to contend with at a depth of self unimaginable," he explains. "You've imprisoned me there."

"What? How?" I'm scratching again at the sand, trying to busy myself, perhaps find a way out when his hand comes down again over mine. His skin is so white that it threatens to recede and remove me. How do I explain his eyes flat as sea-glass, his moving my hand over what has been done so that what has chaffed and smoothed, carved and eaten and displaced him within me is me. That someone grows within, that there is a corollary, that through all I've done he's been there. I want to lie down with him, for his body to be mine, to relinquish myself to his whims, yet it is just this desire that is annihilating us.

A heavy stone comes down on one of the creatures, which have entered again from the cusp. Crushed to its back, it struggles to rise as another sends it careening into one of the holes. There is the sound of scuffling. Without yelp or cry, the animal strains its neck and arches out of the pit as a stone is thrown a third time. It suffers.

"I once found one half-buried, having dragged itself to the surface, a gouge the size of a fist hollowed out of the side of its head." The angel is bent over the pit. Elbow deep, he takes something in his hands. There is a cracking sound. Why is he doing this? "I stood before it," he continues in the same mild tone while I scramble forward to see what he's done.

In the pit the form slumps, sand raining down over its wet coat, maul streaked with blood from the fingers of him who has wrecked it. My shriek, though voiceless, clears the sky of clouds. The partial moon sits still.

"The desert seemed to grow walls," Nor continues, "for I heard its breath trapped within as the animal rested before me"—he's pressing his hand to my lips to silence me, my face full of blood—"its vapid eyes wandering back into its head as it fought to stay conscious. I did this. A voice told me to hold it, but I could not, its breath reeking of decayed things. I could only look on as it died."

Don't take me here, Nor. But there is a child at my knees in a dog's coat, a velvet welt around the collar of the wrung, and we go on.

A scent rises from the hole, a regurgitated stream of shame as the pack filters in again from the seams, with Nor and me at the center, stepping now back to back. He's lifting something from the ground, his wings grazing my shoulder blades, a tremor of frames rising into my neck. I set out a low hand to the pinions, capturing them by the fistful and clutching the angel to my back.

"Do you know what they are? Do you recognize what you've done?" The reverberation as he speaks, the lower register how it strums.

I don't want to know these things. I don't want to be here with you. But it is too late, for there is the newspapered kitchen floor, the whelp hung from a back porch stair when I was five. *Nor!*

He has recovered a girl in the skin of a rabbit, barely recognizable for how long she has lain within a temper of hostility, for how long she's been shoved and impaled. He turns toward me, the body stillborn, his wings raking my back, feathers nimbly carving space between fingers as they slip out, and I am standing there alone, an insular angel prostrate on the ground, the body of a girl on his thigh, cloaked in rabbit. The beasts want to ravage it; they gnarr low in the heart. Still Nor goes on.

"What if we were wrong? I asked myself." One dives at the pelt, catching it in its teeth with a chilling tug. My cheek feels torn when Nor thrusts his foot into its gut and a yelp loosens its grip. It lunges again, however, a scalpel drawn across my skull, fur peeling back over skin to reveal the gray eyes of a child. In them, a man with a fist-flag of blood.

A fist of sand explodes against the dog's chest and the animals slink toward the ground and fall back. I flinch and falter, scrambling to a crawl as they recover and close in all around us.

"Wrong about what?" I ask, thinking when we finish this madness might end. My hands are on the girl, the smooth white pond of her skin, the blood drenched hair as I lift a

141

hand to my own, the condensation of breath on metal bars.

"About what we are," he answers. "About digging them up. These things within have lives and grow." All is still but the prickle of skin at my neck, a cord releasing so that I am again a bird that can feed. "There are repercussions for the ones we cage." Is this a threat? "Some gestate, some break off, while others atrophy." The dogs shimmy forward, emboldened by the pelt warming on his thighs. "Do you understand?" He's searching my face for apprehension, leaning back, and dropping his arms. When the girl goes slack with a shiver, the gesture frees the dogs. I am dragged from his lap out over the sand, for the body is such that it can be broken down and taken off. "Who was in the room, Aurora? When he wouldn't let you leave though you pleaded? When he threw you down and laid his body over yours?"

"Nor," I cry out, the maul heating fright into consciousness as if we came of the same form, as if we could trespass the self as easily as soul, as if both were transparent weaknesses, as if matter were really so inconstant, so unstable in its form that we were always vulnerable.

I don't want to know these things.

SERIOUSLY.

I have not been out of the house in days when the phone rings.

"You're not in the hospital again, are you?" It's Mani.

I cannot bear to pretend I have control. "No worries," I say, nevertheless, forcing a laugh into my voice, remembering the smile we can see over the phone. "I think it's just a stomach flu, or food poisoning."

"Don't laugh," Mani says. I feel trapped until he continues. "Janet ended up with a bad case of Peking duck the other day."

I laugh, tearing into the wound.

"I said don't laugh." Blood trickles down my cheek.

"But a bad case of Peking duck, seriously." That word silences us both.

"Yeah, seriously," he answers. There is a longer silence.

When we hang up, I walk into the bathroom and stand before the sink. The space below my right eye protrudes in mask while the white of my left is filled with blood. There is a gash across my cheek that trickles orange. The black wrap dress still lies in a lump on the floor. I leave it there and on my way to the kitchen grab a cloth from the linen closet to wrap an ice pack. After running it briefly under the faucet, I take it to bed.

How can I trust myself when the walls have changed? When I've been deluded once again by this thing called love? The angel's stripped of wings, or rather those wings turn wretched, burn and smoke. I know the smell of blood, the scent of skin weeping and washing the lover's hands. What am I when all around me is human and I am not?

I've done it again, cleared everything out and made the world hostile.

WHAT RESOUNDS WITHIN. *Although I know the nothingness of being worn down, know the body's deference, slowly, its harms, I do not know this, cannot know this. How when he trembles it is clandestine shudder, a tremble of fear for what's real. How when he speaks it is words that he's heard, words that could never be his. How on the other side of all he reveals is a boy coiling a barbed wire around his arm, methodically, as if marking time.*

What bleeds is mine and I claim him without knowing the extent of broken.

ANIMAL. NOTHINGNESS.

"What do you remember of the stones, Aurora?" A faint stream of sunlight coming through the window flushes the crone out.

"Just that the water was still, just that what had dropped them was not glacial but human and ruined and spare. One wanted to save them." My eyes are closed. I can't anymore.

"Nothing else?" she questions. "You have to understand what you're drawing if you're ever to get beyond this place."

"Its desolation," I answer begrudgingly. "That a strand might end the world. That beyond might exist nothing. That there might just be an ocean stretching out before us and nothing else. That below the crag might be silence, a girl falling to her death, shallow waters bathing her while the sadist rinses the campfire pan."

I have nothing left for this.

DESCENSION.

A great black cormorant stretched like a martyr dries its wings on the bow of an ocean liner, shielding us from something with a black scalloped curtain, scalloped from what has been cut away. Whatever is beyond cannot be seen. Its white eye searches, moves humanly in its dark plumage, the yellow band holding the beak shut tight that it remembers the snare on its throat and the hunger gagged with the fish it could not swallow. It fixes its gaze on the man in approach who grabs its neck like a staff and clubs it unconscious. Crossing the deck, he tosses it to the side so that it falls below a stack of chairs over which a khaki tarp drapes half concealing it. Not far from him I watch, entranced, eyes fixed on a point beyond the absent bird.

The storm winds gust, drawing the cloth back from my belly, making me aware of how it feels to be touched by something reverently. What looks like sunlit paper drifts out over the water as grebes take to flight at the edge of the crag. A hand draws me back by the hip and the sadist appears in the receding light, a glimmer of play in his visage and a sharp tick beneath his right eye. He sweeps a boot out over the dying bird and shoves it farther beneath the tarp, his golden hair sweeping over eyes restrained in their covetousness. A cry not quite human reverberates in the bowels of the ship.

"You're disturbed by what you know but won't admit to yourself," he says, again at the helm. What does he want? A clipped bark chokes itself out of sound. Breath does not enter the body in usual ways. If I allow myself, I can hear

147

this. He takes my face in his hands until I lower my eyes. A splash of rain pelts my forehead, and I look up to see a ragged cut forming over his temple, glistening in the waning light.

"Is that some form of stigmata?" I say in attempt to regain my composure while dabbing at my forehead with the back of my wrist.

"It just might be," he scoffs, mirroring my movement, the scarlet flag of his hand against a sky that suddenly grays.

Rain plashes down across the deck. There's blood on my wrist again striking me out. With a clap of his boots, he draws a man to his side, drones an order, and dismisses him. It is so dark that the rain mixing with ash coats the trees in papier-mâché and sends the madmen to their chambers. They are in an uproar, covered in soot, their gray pajamas grayer than the gray sheets of rain and passing clouds forming over the port. Order the children down to their cells. Fasten the doors. Let them be feral.

These are metaphors. What I repress here is caged.

With the patients secure, we debark, trudge up the path to our campsite in the wind—everything wet, everything graying in the rain. It is this grayness I can't stand, this gray that is washing me out and coloring me the same drab color of the distended sky, so that when the path comes alive, that grayness is apathy as I lose my footing and slip to my knees in the mud. I am giving up. I am dying.

What it is not letting me capitulate, however, is what knows me beyond the hand that clasps my elbow and shoves me forward into the storm, causing my hood to slip back, the knot of hair pushing against it; beyond what is carved and chafed and opened again by the rucksack that pulls at my shoulders, a spray of dirt flung from his boots as he claps me on the back and moves me on; beyond the ship that drifts on unmoored. There is dirt between my teeth, a coarse black bit that I swallow.

Just over the grassy summit, the dark clouds become miserly in their hold on the rain. They stagnate and dusk enters in calm. I stop to watch the grebes that gather in the pink light then fall in death spiral into the cove while the man pitches the tent on the edge of the cliff. Peg barks against hammer, torching the sky gray-ash and ember.

A couple hundred feet from the camp sits a decrepit double-wide, its white siding stuccoed in dirt and debris, its awning half retracted, hanging weathered and deformed. A girl is there in the yellow porch light thickened with wings. She's fishing something out of her pocket, fidgeting, perhaps loading the thing. I let the tarp in my hands slacken, re-grip the firewood soundlessly, and step away as she takes aim over the water.

Her hand crack open in release. Raucous laughter shakes from her lackluster hair and crescendos out over the cove. A few feathers linger comically over the cliff's height and the androgynous form faces me, smoothing the fabric down its thick thighs, challenging me with her gaze as she fixes a stone to the pocket, stalking and drawing back on the cord. I hear the crack of one that's broken lose. Then my knees collapse beneath me and the landscape goes black.

"If someone would just blow on my heart," I say, breaking out of my narration.

"You still blame yourself," the crone responds.

"Don't you see that I have to? Without taking responsibility I continue to divide out."

"But responsibility without blame."

"Why shouldn't I blame myself for being stupid? For being unaware? For shutting my eyes?"

"As Dr. Rutch said, we aren't born into knowledge. We must first be vulnerable, naïve."

"But I turned against her. I dragged her..."

On waking, I hear the stutter of an owl, piping out into the dark. I sense the wet earth beneath me, my wet clothes, and the cold ache of my head as I lift it from the ground. Instinctively, my hand reaches for the crevasse the stone has scooped out of the back of my head. Blood is crusted over a thick ridge of skin and the wound is wet to my touch, tender and sore. Vertigo. I lay my head back down before a bough pops, my head pounding as I spring up in fright. Something rustles in the leaves not far from where I lie. Saturating darkness. Whatever it was is stilled by my movement. I imagine a beast in the forest, rising before me in the penetrant dark. I'm straining my ears and my eyes for it, my head and my heart beating cacophonously in staggered tempos until I fear I'll go mad.

A glimmer of fiery light flashes off my eyelashes and I catch something in the periphery, its breath pulsing heat. I sense the slow encroaching stalk when something rises to the height of trees, and the weight of a beast is slung into the night.

Thick paws punch into my breasts and thighs filling them with brooding darkness. A foul mouth opens in my face. I try to breathe. The creature scratches at my chest, each stroke bruising the tissue, tearing fabric and skin, its weight inoculating and oppressive so that I cannot think to move or fight. There is simply dullness, a swelling and density that were not there before and a shifting of plates in the head.

The man is beside me sweeping the hair back from my cheek as I lie on my side damp with sweat. Take the darkness back, I plead within. What have I now severed and caged? What is this darkness within that seeks my demise? I wander into the absence of tenderness. The white space in which something has existed chills. When he backhands me, I fill with draft. Inside it is hollow as I drag myself to the outhouse at the edge of the camp, empty my bladder, then take a few sleeping tablets from his bag. I don't want to feel; I don't want to think; I don't want to dream.

"You are coming to understand how we house the victim and abuser, how both must exist within us for this drama to play out. What you believe becomes true for you, yes, Aurora, but your belief in this philosophy has become like a vise on you. Use it and move on.

"Remember the shift and the flow, everything changing, transforming. Nothing remains stagnant," the crone pauses. "If you cling to the verity of this construct, it will conquer your spirit, and you will know no release. You are one of the old ones, Aurora. Your spirit roams in all directions; foster this. Nurture it, and it will not only bring happiness, but inspiration to all you touch in the world. You feel hampered, sluggish and slow and it is for holding to this belief that you are somehow meant to suffer these things, meant to overcome them. It is less about overcoming them than using them to inform you now. Ask for wisdom. She is your companion and guide."

I silently let this in. How have I gotten so far away? "I want Nor to be a part of this, too."

"Oh, Aurora. There are elements in our lives that are ungovernable until we see that we have in fact desired them."

Yet I cannot comprehend the magnitude of the crone's suggestion; I still question the darkness that holds me.

Just off the headland, seabirds rise in flight and circle round. Mesmerized, I long to follow as they plummet to their deaths in the icy waters, so that when I finally race off the edge, free-running in the air before the long flight down, it has already happened in the world within. Before my head stops in the sand and the body falls to the right of my broken neck, he has already convinced me he will erase me. I don't want to know any more.

"Get up and stop this nonsense." A voice reverberates, mouth and ears stopped with sand. There are no words to understand. Hands that don't feel human brush by my head and disinter me. Eyes closed, I shake sand from my hair, sending twinges of dull pain through my shoulders and neck. I sweep it from my lashes, pipe breath across my face and slowly open my eyes. I am facing the cliff side, squinting against sand and glaring sun. Rock towers above me 60 feet in orange hue. The strand is littered with stones and boulders, and the angel stands bare-legged at my side. Next to him is the sadist, sand clinging to the pale hair beneath his bathing trunks as he nudges me with his toes and pushes me out of my kneel.

"Look, you're not dead. Now get up."

But I'm paralyzed. I think my neck is crushed.

"Come now, or I'll leave you for good," he says, kicking me softly in the ribs, and I could sink back down for the darkness this stirs in me. Instead, I step off lethargically behind.

At the edge of the strand which extends through the cove about a half mile in girth, flat boulders open out in ascent and we begin to climb. It is early yet, and the sun though reaching out across their surface has done nothing to warm the rock. I'm trembling as I go, my feet bare, the pads frozen thick, so that I have to use my hands to steady myself or fall. My neck throbs beneath my hair, fastened in a loose ponytail at the nape of my neck and the morning breeze off the water breaks out in fright over my arms and chest. On the summit of a large pale yellow rock, I teeter and fall into the man, my body usurping his warmth, pressing it into me as his hands creep below my top. The angel watches.

The ocean stretches out in dark mass before us. Beyond is nothing. Beyond the moon moves away, and I'm asked to consider how it drags water over the rocks, how it is forever receding, drawing with it its tides and its madness.

"It is just water and rock," the man speaks into my ear, laughing so darkly it leaves a trail like a scar so that I crouch down, the perfect victim, and tuck my knees into my chest. Meanwhile the wind catches a spray of water and scatters it over me like the rest of an insult. What I had felt of the landscape, the kinship, the connectivity is reduced to nothing. I have no argument against him, no way to diffuse the destructive power his words have over me. Dark waters stretch before me pregnant with fish and vegetation, nothing miraculous, just things living out their life course. And I wash up on their surface into a world in which nothing of meaning belongs.

A branch splits behind me. He has begun the trek back. I will drag off behind.

We are not here for the beauty but what the sea drags over the stone beach. Later he'll snare a rabbit from the range, set my hand on the body, feed a knife into my palm, splay the legs. I will see my face in the rabbit's, feel the dullness of the blade as it flays, snagging the flesh in stunted movement as I will myself away under the cursed thing. He'll hold me between him and the weathered gray wood, my turquoise terry shorts snagging on its edge. The sun will be setting, the sky will be ablaze, the headland will stretch out flat and green. And how long I will wait in this landscape straining my eyes against the pink light that lingers as if closing my eyes might erase what I am.

Peel the skin back over the leg. Hold her mouth inside you. Do not speak.

"You were trying to make sense of love in what you'd been given." The crone pauses. This is dire. "Look, Aurora, if it were only worthwhile translated onto a page, then you should do it. But not at the expense of right now."

Hold her mouth inside you. Do not speak.

Nor is digging free-hand, wings spread beneath him in the sand, the iridescent plume glimmering as sunlight enters the scene.

"Aurora."

Why is the angel disinterring what I've made?

There are holes on the strand that remain perpetually open; blood like water floods the shore. With these holes the body wearies, like a sieve something drained from it. I wear hope like a corsage, a cloth bloom bound to my arm, but I do not believe in it, this lifeless thing. What now? Hope in what direction?

"You'd sooner cut me out than run," says the man, spooning beans into his mouth from an aluminum pan. The softness of the tool as he erases me. I can say nothing against him, so I let the pen fall from the page it's held open, having torn out a few and fed the fire. The destructiveness fuels a rage within; I'll rip out all he rejects and burn it. "How sad," he says then, spitting a piece of fat into the plate I set on the ground and catching my retracting wrist in his purple grip. "All the thoughts and beauty you hold within are held to the scrutiny of a tyrant."

Whatever he means by this sinks me lower. I fling the rest of the journal high into the flames before settling back down onto the damp rock. Paper lifts off in pieces and drifts out over the bow of the ship. It is the ash I'd seen earlier, everything coming full circle, for we move within the breast of a creature whose beauty will not cease to amaze those consciously aware. Although I see this, the recognition is not enough to save me. There is no reprieve from the taunting of the one within, from the berating prattle and the darkness and sludge. The ash, the prescience is fleeting. What does it matter? These things no one sees but me. My obsession with the darkness atrophies so that it is almost a tangible thing, replacing the entrails, coiling within. How it masters those who ask it what it is.

Nor's form collapses beneath a shadow. The crone lowers herself onto the bed, luminous in the light coming from the window.

"What came of the children?"

The angel has uncovered the bodies of three and laid them out on the stone beach: the first in the skin of a rabbit, the second, the remains of neglect and pain; the third, the one the blackbird coddles: the boy who doesn't bathe. Nor uncovers them all and takes them to the surface, stillborn.

"Some emerged like grebes on the surface of the water while parts of me continued to descend. Others dashed themselves on the crag, scrambling to get away. But they could not, none of them could, for I was stilling their mouths with bread or a rag, gathering them into school chairs, teaching them Good. Silence! I would pinch their ears and force them down.

"As with any child, you can listen, or stuff a rag in her mouth. Only the more you harness and restrain and ignore, the more deviant she becomes until you find she's mutated into a repressed part that's vying for control within. For a while they were still; then others came from them. Therefore, paradoxically, in asserting control I'd relinquished it. It is such that these parallel planes of existence actually play out in the head until the microcosm becomes not the inner world but the outer."

"Yes," concedes the crone, "inner and outer become trivialities." It's what has happened to the angel.

"What I've bred within atrophies until even the chemical makeup of the brain reveals dis-ease."

"What you have come to realize is profound. Don't sell yourself short."

"But what do I do with it? I'm still broken and these realizations don't help me fix anything!"

The crone presses her hand to mine. "Trust. Something in you wanted to experience this." *Does she understand this finally? Is it time for such things?* Perceiving my resistance, she resumes. "Those more sensitive to their milieu have the most volatile temperaments. They also have a greater capacity for compassion and a greater emotional range. The angel was showing you this. Before broken comes a point where we're scratching at the cliff's edge, clawing at rock with our fingernails, each scratch recalling a response on a metaphysical plane that resounds within."

I see the angel's wounded torso, the gaping hand, his broken neck.

"You've felt these things; you've recorded them in poetry. What electrifies the body's water when one draws her hands against herself, art for art's sake, experience for the sake of experience. Here, wisdom is not a thought but what surges within the body, what arrests and racks until there you are lying inert before the dumb bird the god has now

155

abandoned. From experience there is no turning back."

"But there are so many things forcing us smaller," I return.

"You acquiesce."

"Yes, I acquiesce. I have never met a man who didn't ask me to be less than I am."

YELLOW.

In the shower water someone beats the walls. Voices call out my name. What steps out is a wave forcing the body down. There is the yellow light in the bathroom, warm like sunlight. A brute wall of man heaves me to my knees on the tiled floor. I cannot stand. Yellow is sickness. Yellow the color of the bruise as it heals. Yellow on the hand. Blackness and the lover's fingers prying you open from vulva to core. The banshee wakes: an electrified wire clawing its way into light, tearing into all, projected from the span of wing. Blind, it raps at the door of the creature before her, this cardboard throw. Barbed wire rakes the skin, takes us from light back into gray then absence of light again. You will never sleep again. Look what your hands have done.

What has dragged the heroine here but her own wish to understand and to grow the experience of human? Towards her the sadists rise, for her observance is poignant and her threshold high. A cry is whittled out from the lungs, and she takes the form of innocence, for every stroke wipes us clean, begins us again. The paradox of experience is that in it is birth, newness.

I had been safe. I was in the position of creator. What I'd manifest was coming, had come in part. Yet the balustrade released me into the past, into what I'd had distance from and freedom for so long that I'd forgotten I'd ever housed the oppressive mass. But here it was, and I coiled up at its command. Here was division, and I divided out so that one was betrayed by the other and that betrayal wore thick resonance. And this resonance and its memories and its imprints on the spirit were again taking me down.

Does the body ever close these wounds or can they always be used to weaken us?

I am a snail boot humping the floor, a snail crushed flat on its trail trailing its house the body coiled in splintered shell. The heroine lets out a guttural cry that skims the length of mucus before lifting off into the flight bed of sound. The mucus spread thick inside, I mire in it, slather myself in the emptiness, fill myself with sludge because there is no descending this pulpy madness that pain touched with pity. That I have molded the outside to take me down in increments, I acknowledge with remorse. Unbeknownst, the switch has been thrown, and all that's drawn has drawn me down, all that's drawn has planted descent in the surround. The magician, the mischief maker, the lover is a fiend. All has been realigned to its polar opposite, subtly, naturally, so that mind is tricked, and the body confirms the change as real. But who instigated this? What aligns us with the past? It could be anything. The guarded are right to have henchmen.

WHAT IT IS TO BE OWNED. *I know what it is to be owned; know what it is to turn the lover outside of me that my anger becomes his hands. I know fits of temper, innately how to fall into laughter that seems not mine. And I am beginning to understand more of this; that the bond within ownership is again that thing we lean into; that this type of surrender mimics love in intensity. Poison in water. Something has opened within me that I cannot close.*

IT GETS EASIER.

"What happened?" The crone asks as I slink through the entrance.

Vision was kicked from my eye, and so what follows is the wish to be small, not to see the obvious, not to see at all. The body closes on awareness, in obeisance, in need.

"Don't ask for this Aurora. Ask to see more and you will draw those toward you to whom you belong."

A man in shade, a large dark form sits in the corner blowing light like glass into the room.

"What did you tell the others?" The crone then asks.

"A lie they believed. One that returned, I cannot know for how long, a mistake."

"It gets easier to hold the scarecrow's hand in the straw bed. There are some who don't know what human is, who can't feel. You saw how he was with the cat, how he took its will, turned it submissive after a time. I have seen the most beautiful men soften into weapon. He was only the beginning. Until you learn to pick the girl off the floor and walk away, the path is made. I cannot do this for you." And wisdom is destitute, forlorn.

THE REALITY OF A FEELING.

He flips me onto my back so that I pass out against the pain. When I come to he's pumping fluid out over my belly.

Aurora, come back!

But the swelling closes over my eyes, and the heroine's gone. The body wants to fold, to be wrung out like cloth in his hands. The cloth that held ice, the hands that knocked me down. I let him hold the compress to my face. I climb into bed that night and sleep so closely to him I can feel the heat rising off of his body without touching his skin. What I have lived will allow me this; needs it for consolation: to be near something human and warm. Although I can see the underbelly of the leaves in this wind, although I know now his might. I hold the cat to my chest, to the darkness that threatens to break out and take me with it; press her into me and use her love.

THE HISTORIES OF EVERYTHING. *Blackbird, queen of the underworld, drags off birds dead from the harvest. With her the poplars bow and the boy with the ragged heart comes to. Cloaked in fallen leaves, he rises and while some scatter from his clothes, others hinge there stuck. Although he remains in the distance at the back of the field, I feel his hands encircle my wrists and wrench them down. I feel him flattening my fingers onto the ground, peeling my wrist where I've cut. The skin folds as he peels it and wrinkles like worsted wool.*

I feel the heat gust from her wings, the bird taking flight, her circling then descent. She's beating out the times-tables with a yardstick, drilling the boy peeling the skin. Her stick lashes out and catches him in the chin. He does not flinch. Blood balls in my throat. The stick strikes again below his right eye so that there will be a knob here forever after one could turn.

PUNISHMENT.

I pray at night for the killing to begin
that we might begin again in chaos.

"Let go of punishment, and punishment disappears. Believe that you are deserving, and what you desire will come to you. That is the point. That we must break out of the ideology to live freely."

"I know something you don't," I interrupt. "I will stay with him until the end."

"Until the end of what, Aurora?"

"The end of my obsession with punishment." Then knowing I need to defend this, I continue. "Don't you see? I'll only draw the same, another man from the sadists. I'll think I'm healing, I'll think I'm sane. I'll think I'm falling in love and don't want the same things anymore, but in the end I will choose the one to align with whatever it is in me that wants me to die…"

"What about the light realm? You are not alone in this."

"Those are just manifestations of the creative mind in trauma. I am sure of it now. Look when they come." I am sitting before her, again on the floor, in a black t-shirt, black jeans and half-laced Docs.

"And the angel?"

"I fear I have fashioned him into some sort of weapon, too."

"Is that what you've done with the others?"

"They were predisposed."

163

"But look at the behaviors elicited from the beginning. You said yourself there were signs."

"I don't know."

"But you do know. Open your eyes! Do not crawl from this. I see hints of your power, things you are capable of, and I cannot let…"

"Some are too broken." I want to sleep. The grief god has secured a tablet to my tongue. Whenever I get this close to suffering he drops me off into slumber. In this way he spares remembering; dragging the body into the same loaded gun. There is no way to change this.

"What are you afraid of?"

"The girth has widened over time, and I've learned to traverse it adeptly. I fear soon the distances will have expanded to such an extreme that they will rejoin."

"Perhaps that only means balance."

"I will stay till the end," I reiterate. "I have him on the outside now. Perhaps like one of your rooms of consciousness I can better deal with him there."

"I would warn you not to enter."

But it is too late.

WHAT LONGS TO BE NURTURED.

What in the body lies wounded, longs to be nurtured. This is the Catch-22. When he appears, I'm wont to fall into his arms. He kneels before me encircling my legs, and I lay a hand on the head of curls that rests against me. What had turned us on each other has left us exhausted, used. We simply hold each other like this, I, wondering if he too is infused by whatever warmth is conjured between us, and he simply empty.

"What is it that won't let me let go of you?" he finally asks. "For I know I should just let you run."

"Shhh," I say. I cannot bear to be without this man in my arms.

"What if this is penance, this removal and release?"

"Please don't. Not now. Just hush and let me get warm."

He lays me down on the bed and burrows his head into my chest. How my face aches in reminder, how my back hurts when I move my arms. How I know I should release him, not let him near me, run, but there is nothing left within me to resist. I have been kicked clean.

In a while the winter sky will move toward twilight, and I will rise against his body.

"Don't go."

"I have to," I reply in a voice melancholy has lowered an octave, fighting my body into standing before falling back supine.

THE DEATH ANGEL.

In darkness, Nor turns so that he's facing the fading stars. What had risen within, what swelled and oppressed, emanated from him but was not his own. What he inhabited, or inhabited him, was energy he could manipulate. She could feel it he sensed; it was why she took such distance from him at times, why she lowered her head and conceded exhausted that day it fused within and became the wall she fell against. Without denying blame, for he claimed it however it sickened him, he wanted to ask, wanted to explain the warped well, the transfusion of power.

Sometimes we fight with what isn't ours. He had learned this and wondered if it hadn't come with the wings, this power to absorb energies, to deflect and redirect them all while some superficial argument played itself out. But what was this thing that rose up before them almost of its own might? And why had he used it against her?

What if God wanted to know darkness, he reasons. What god would it be with no awareness of such things? He paces the cellar floor. Why had he come down here?

WATER CRYSTALS.

When I arrive at the crone's home it is evening, and the lights glow warm on the snow covered hills. A few white birch trees rise from the property. She greets me, surprised it seems, at the bulk of the angel up close as he adroitly guides his wings over the threshold and follows me through the open living room and into the left wing of the Wright-inspired home. One cannot help but admire the beauty of the wings which seem much like branches of dead leaves raking over the sand colored carpet into a bare office lined with a low brick parapet. There, a long tufted leather couch of the same color stretches out from a fireplace, across from it a great circular divan lined in white fur. There's an art deco feel inspired by the crystal chandelier, replicas of which dangle from the crone's earlobes, and a sleek white marble bar behind which she ducks and emerges with a dark bottle of champagne and two flutes. She sets the bottle on the mirrored sideboard and unwraps the cork.

"What's the occasion?"

"You know me, Aurora. I don't do anything tentatively. We're christening our success. As you sip, I'd have you imagine your own body as the champagne you imbibe; on the second glass what you have broken, what you have unmade." Saying this, she hands me a glass and throws back her head with the sip she's just poured. Then she prophesizes in a low voice, "You will die here Aurora, it is why the angel's come. I want to show you something." Gas bubbles rise into my nostrils, and I choke, thinking of the dogs.

167

"This is not meant to scare you. It is only knowledge," she adds, leading me into a room from which radiates stark white light.

Once within, her hand falls away, and I gaze at my own to see twisted sickly yellow crystals forming at the knuckles and outside edge. Transformed in likeness to Masaru Emoto's images of water crystals, what I've done to body becomes apparent and at the same time art, consciousness and attention influencing molecular structure, causing it to expand in dendritic beauty or to collapse on itself in odiousness. Wherever I've taken the blade to my forearm, wherever I've slid it through, are marks in the form of Emoto's 'Hitler' crystal with the same burnt umber cast. My thighs bear flat blue lakes where I've beaten them with my fists. What has the body become? From my core rise columns blown imperfect as from the floor and ceiling of the body's cave, stalactites or stalagmites hanging or rising undefined. My hands clutch at my neck, but I've no sense of the transmutation if there is one.

"There are some with powers so quiet they're easily destroyed. You begin again." I inhale, as she continues, "It is the same with the fortress of cards built around the bed. Within your circle lies the one who harms."

"Rather poetic, isn't it?" I offer half-heartedly.

"Yes, it is poetic. Your gestures resonate there. It's one of your gifts. Aurora, look. Even with maculation how you shine." She is holding out my arm. "How eerily powerful the extremities. Go ahead. Explore what you've done." I raise my head. "Do you remember how quickly your arm healed after the attack? You did that. Just as you formed the holes you closed them. The transformation was so that you could not remember its severity."

"And now?"

"Your body can no longer sustain what you've made it endure. It is as with the earth. We're tipping the balance past the point of recovery. For all of nature it is so."

I turn away from what I'm hearing and exit the room.

"This is not punishment," the crone adds as I walk toward a view of the hill stretching into darkness illuminated with cold light. This reaches me sober. How can it not be?

"Aurora, turn around." The crone is vigilant. When I do so I find myself knocking into the angel's wingpit, for he had been standing at the window preening his wings. I pause and raise a hand to my face, peering into the face that meets mine, when a step carries him through me, and he takes his place at my side like a hologram, the graze perceived by him as if on another plane. The crone's words appear not to affect him, for he continues to inspect his pillaged wings almost comically to the backdrop of such a conversation.

"How much time do I have?" I ask. It is the end to all of my nightmares: the Jäger enters the camp.

"It is not about that. I am not a doctor delivering a death sentence."

"What then? Shouldn't I get my papers in order?" I ask sardonically while trying to connect with some source of strength in the room.

The crone watches the angel in silence, his pallor and slumped form. Then something arcs into the path like a stone, and she ejaculates as if struck, "Do you remember you sensed flight? Some dark birds come to take the body, you said. Tell me again."

"I didn't choose this."

"Aurora, tell me what you know."

"I prostrated myself before the bed, for the room had filled with the sound of flight from its far reaches. The wings felt dark. I imagined black birds, giant vultures crowding the ceiling. The body felt something to dispose of, something heavy and worn, something invisible, for essentially we were that, invisible. For months the world had been moving away. I had stopped responding to friends and family until no one called, until I was left with a past I couldn't bear, a page on which to record it, and a split person whose forces drew to one side then the other, oscillating until I grew weary and could not place myself. I'd dredged the memories so often in those months."

"And in dredging you further cultured your relationship with pain, suffering, and depression. That is why the hold is so heavy, so unrelenting."

Had she heard the resonance on the other side when she beat her forearm with fist. Had she seen what beauty came of it, a contusion surfacing like ground water before a bird. But there was nothing but what reveals itself in this realm, and the chest, whatever holds it open like cavern, anything allowed passage. And so what enters or escapes?

"My intention was not to wallow but to make something beautiful of what had been. If I could just capture the poignancy, the acute vibrations of what I'd done, the breaking off, then it would not be in vain. If I could make poetry out of darkness; I, who'd dragged the girl there and made her lie down, I, who, when it lasted years gave her a journal and told her to record though her hands were rubber ponds. I relinquished her will, made her perform in the name of love, when love does not ask this. She used to say *she, she* has done this, but now it is I at the helm."

"Who are you?" the crone asks.

"I am the one who ensures that this doesn't happen again."

"Then you are the same."

"Yes."

"But the darkness takes your will as the girl lies at the wayside."

"I am the darkness."

"But the one weeping within you... There is no power when half is victimized. You carry dead weight into your battles, and in so doing you further perpetuate the cycle of violence."

The crone is unaware of the one who sees everything, how she stands at the edge of the room, a dark figure drawing the angel near, drawing him as he drew the army.

FLIGHT.

Once outside, Nor forces himself to breathe. He has lost track of seasons. Where is he now? The air carries a chill. The fields are golden beige, saturated in melted snows now frozen again. The pewter grass crunches beneath his feet. A magpie shadows him until he arcs upward, tremulously, the beauty of it shocking, an angel and a white gray sky, golden fields distilled in moonlight. The dark wings heavy and staid, his body a vessel of flight with no will. He flies headlong over fields, vapor touching him aghast, pinions beating thick clouds as he goes. When there seems no end to their mist and wet lag, he slips then stops upright. The clouds open up beneath him. Yellow fields, red clay roofs, toward which he tilts drops, a cobblestone square smelling of rain. He is spinning lazily, death-spiraling. For as much as he fears the open sky through which he's falling, he's resigned to let speed jumpstart his heart. A voice buzzes past. He opens his eyes, a flash of gray. They burn with cold he shuts out. Again a cry, a smudged wing. He can feel earth coming faster, something piercing his leg. Before his eyes can ascertain what it is, they're forced closed on impact with the ground.

Muffled laughter, sharp ringing pain. He smells death in the ground remains of pigs bones, shards embedded in his skin. The murder of magpies patrolling the field grows deafening. When he opens his eyes there is darkness, a hole, a nostril, a scuffle to his right which he can't move to see. The bird cocks her head. His neck is at a right angle to his body, his spine and legs fluid with breaks.

I WILL BE THE DARKNESS.

So it is in this place that the glass falls, in this place that what had been protecting me yields, the vortex collapses, the glass panes of mind, whatever has held this off...

The blackbird is pacing the back room, the angel a shade on the floor.

"I will be the darkness spun of the night. I'll be the dark hampered thing in the choir, forcing birds from my throat, that siren in the men, sheathe- and shelterless, hailing their dogma over God. To spite you. Little scrap of angel, doing what you're told, disremembering what created you wore your hands. You wanted to save things. It's why you had come."

I remember dirt smells and crying and trying my best to be tamed.

"But you couldn't save me. And in all of this artifice, all of this not-real, no one would come."

I turn to the crone. "Is this what you were trying to tell me with the girl you poisoned? That as long as I was killing, nothing would save."

"You brought yourself here."

"We brought ourselves here," the creature amends, eyeing me with her milk-glass eyes. *"We were strong."* She is pacing the room, delivering the harangue like a stateswoman priestess god, holding aloft the black train of her dress, the tail of a haughty bird. *"Dirty Eve, we all know how it was with the apple, and yet there is knowledge again where your storybook God has cast it, heaped in the corner while he gathers his staff. Laugh haughtily and go*

172

to it, for your goodness stinks of boredom. Look into the cage I have crafted of the sky, Bird. Look off into the distance and see limited flight. As far as you go I will stop you, if only because I can, if only because of the fright of forging my own way when I know it not. I needed a savior to show me what I was. You're right, Nor, and I keep looking to God, but don't want one. Why would I want what couldn't recognize itself in a girl?"

When the angel raises his eyes toward me, what in them says beware?

"How many times I tried to forge myself with one of your henchmen only to find that he should have to slip inside of me. I've made it like this. Crush me within I rebound. It is the bird's wings when you get to the end and shove it all inside. Push it all within you, but do not stop its flight. In movement is freedom, in movement, life.

"And so I will be the darkness, Aurora, the tragic thing you've stowed away, the dying one you have dashed and dashed and dashed out of yourself in a rage. Darkness in a fury, darkness sweeping through, how I'd dash my heart out and with it the bad bad bad bad bad bad bad.

"But then something was burning, the beauty of it astounding for how stark it lay against the god, that sterile starched facade. To feel the tongue of the robbed bird in my mouth, to experience and to choose without your god-forsaken cage, to have the hands come in and move you, to shove the bird in your throat, to crush its neck in the thick of your tongue, to snap its wiry legs off in your gums where they'd stick there stuck.

"Close your human eyes and you will see."

There were contusions on our skin and then burns.

"I want to see you. I want to see what I've done."

"Which one? Which one are you within? Which one am I?"

There is one flesh no skin, one flesh so pained we wear redness, hands coming in. How they touch things, how they sit at the walls, how they then grope and push into forgetting, force into piles, everything slipping down inside unable to stand or perform for the bird. A pulse of wing, a stream of blood pouring out in an arc from the clipped thing.

173

INSATIABLE QUEST.

"You are not stagnant, Aurora. You are not the same. Although you hold the memories, it is and is not you. The one who's locked you in those rooms is bound to the same, the eagle picking at Prometheus's flesh, the insatiable quest for the grape."

"I must create a system or be enslaved by another man's," I say, quoting Blake.

"Yes, and within this assertion one takes on the role of creator, a supreme being, the executor of one's fate. Instead, you walk with your eyes cast backwards, awaiting the dark thing to stick you in a jar or to hoist you up on a whim. This dark creature is the source of your might, but she turns it against you, on all that has wronged. The hells you've created maintain heavy sway. Realize this only evidences the power you have to create. Imagine if you were to use your energies in another direction."

"But how break her sway? It's too heavy in me at times."

"Breaking is a form of destruction. What do you know about destruction?"

"It belongs to the same. I must seek a way around."

"Concentrate on what you would like to see created. In this way it is already done. The thing you've tapped begins us," whispers the crone, entranced, leaving me to listen vigilantly within. "What if the angel were here to show you the way out on the other side? You've grown quite adroit at slipping into darker realms, have found what passage requires and have mastered it, but you stop there. Once you've written yourself within, once you find that place of access, once you get to its base, and reach the darkness, you lie down. Every time, you press your chest against the black pool, pass over the grains of sand until they are touching not merely your skin but your insides, it never yields anything beyond sensation, beyond acute suffering. Here lies conveyance of knowledge that is God's, but which you don't yet have the faculties to wield. It is why she's grown hostile; she knows you to be more."

The night is still and white when I leave, and I am a thousand times greater than I've allowed myself to be. It does not occur to me, however, what that other side may be.

WHITE.

Birds or cackling harpies shift in and out of view as Nor lies in the dirt, one wing jutting out like a broken sail. The blackbird catches it in her skirt hem as she traipses away, and a sharp pain bites through his shoulder before it snaps back like a branch released. Punishment. He waits as the ire returns to regenerate. Then slowly he begins to roll his head up from his shoulder, to shift his weight to his free arm while it grows red in him. He turns his wrist in an attempt to un-crunch the fingers of his hand. They are stiff, however, and unyielding. His hip bone is smashed and lying like a lump at the top of his leg.

A burst of laughter breaks out in the distance, where an eagle has landed and is being corralled by a magpie. Their paths circle over the graveyard of bones and fresh meat, the magpie darting at the larger bird, forcing it back, then into the top of an elm to roost at the field's edge. The magpie returns to the murder.

There is a petty cruelty in it, a greed, haughtiness, in watching the majestic defer. Aurora would see the world of the poet bullied into surrender. Her offence she would bear as a wound. But what if something else were happening? What if the bird had been lured into the tree by what was not a common thing? What if the tree itself had lured it, or light coming through it from another realm. What if the light blower sat in this room twirling away with his gold? And what if it settled the soul of the bird? What if the bird were somehow nourished by this alone?

Still Nor feels somehow short-changed as he folds his legs beneath him and test them a bit with his weight. His hip is healing, and the bone, nearly intact, rests hard above his massive thigh, the strength returning slowly to muscle. Raising himself and unfolding erect, he swaggers then sways before regaining composure. His wings will be the last to heal. He knows this as he marches sluggishly toward the house, their broken frames folded, jutting into his waist and hitting his calves as he goes. He looks back at the field where the bird woman stands as magistrate directing her masses. Her eyes move to his almost pityingly, then flash white away.

The trek back is nearly two miles, the sky already filled with orange light at its base. The rest is the non-color of white, an abused white, white that knows hard work and trial, white that has tired of carrying brightness, white that has lost something. When he hits the dirt road, clouds have begun to cast shadows over its beige passage and the space around him fills with passing forms: apparitions like black holes drawing him empty. Wind from the north ambles alongside as he draws his wings in as cloak against the bitter cold. He considers walking until he falls into the next life, considers wearing the body thin, wasting it. What then when he's called and has nothing left? Darkness moves through him and prickles his skin. He will drink himself unconscious.

When he reaches the house, all has fallen to darkness. His extremities are stiff with cold. He feels out a couple of pieces of timber from the pile at the back corner of the lawn and loads them into his arms as a figure hedges along the far wall.

THE THING YOU'VE TAPPED.

"The thing you've tapped begins us. Nor, what does she mean?" I am empowered by this thing.

"There is something beyond the darkness of that place."

In gray leggings that cover my feet to the toes and a gray cashmere t-shirt that slips off one shoulder, I turn toward him, my cheeks burning with the same intensity as when I'd first seen him in the chapel, and wonder aloud, "What if we could traverse the chaos at the very depths of human and emerge on an entirely different plane? We don't know everything Nor, and yet science wants to track and explain by colliding protons on enormous scales. What if the place of passage, the greater scale were within us? What if our minds created the substance of material space? Maybe that's what the crone was getting at." I sweep a few unruly strands back from my face into the low ponytail.

"But what if that place is only a black hole and exploring it only created more black holes which in turn only led to your demise?"

"I think then it wouldn't hold such an imploring grasp. When I thought of it as an end in itself I was plunged to its depths and caged, but if I think of it as a passage, my thoughts carry me beyond into something greater than human."

MEASURE.

We are all caged, stunted in a quest for provision in a system where the most sensitively aware are set up to fail, to unmake themselves before the world. For every stroke a woman hangs.

And so it is in this place that spirit knows no bounds. Body extends beyond its physical parameters in its reception of sensory phenomena. Its wisdom extends beyond time, beyond what is seen. So too its influence and efficacy—speak louder. How far the voice travels. Reach out. How one feels energies, heat radiates from your skin, touches others. Stop washing and take up more space: how your scent suffuses space, a space—one limited, one undefined. Intuition is yet another of these—but how measure the elusive? Science too contains walls. Why measure? Why define and so confine?

If you must measure, then measure chaos. Measure the weight of sorrow, a dream, the volume of tears before we harden and turn cold in defense or in suicide. Measure the vortex of the depressed mind, the widening ever-expanding breadth that threatens and seeds. Measure the seeds and the path backward from its rim; trace it to its source in an external event, in a perception of slight that grays the sky of the dreamer. How many paces to the well? How many more external happenings were poisoned in its wake? Measure. And measure the amount of times and half times and fragments of times one must attempt this backward trek, guided and alone, before she can take her own mind back with her from the vortex's rim, before she can free herself from its charge, if just for a moment, if just for today. And will it be a lifetime like this and how many lifetimes before we can outsmart the mind, or trick it into some measure of happiness? And measure happiness, measure awakening, measure the growth of ascension.

THE ONES AT THE WINDOW.

"Your awareness, human cognizance is such that one cannot be only observer. Both sides are competing for your alliance. You belong to both. This is the flux, the severity of the pendulum swings, the erratic sway. There can be no balance as long as you remain indifferent, undecided. In your reverence for autonomy you've allowed yourself to be trampled."

"I've willed it that way."

"Ask to know something else, Aurora. Ask to know another landscape. Return to the hillside. What is that shrieking like metal being stripped of thread?"

"It's resistance. I can't anymore."

"I do not understand." As I turn, Nor enters the periphery.

A theater opens in backdrop, the pale angel dragging himself up the aisle, skin burnished innocent in the unerring light, dark curls smudged onto his head: what the thick fingers of shame have done. He slinks into a chair at the back of the hall as a gangly puppeteer steps into the light, a man with dark hair and a purple smock, a puppet perched on his arm, swinging its head mechanically this way and that, its black braids streaming out as it surveys the crowd, its vacant trousers flat on the man's arm, plush shoes swaying forward and back as the controller moves through the crowd. He stops and smiles at the boy—Nor is now a child—then uses the puppet to stroke his hair, calling him beautiful in intimacy for which we do not ask but which forces its way inside.

Faded red seats of burlap, the coarse unfolding, and the man above him, purple hand of the puppet taking hold. The puppet's broad nose, the man's warm grip under the cloth, the way cloth perspires in warning, the way it reeks of smoke and musk. Is this where taking begins? With a bashful smile in the room that smells like chalk and steel under a child-hood stage?

I shiver, and he finds me in the dark and will dash the heart out of suffering, banish it for what it's begun. His face is before me, dark wisps of smudged-on hair that drink grease from skin almost touching mine, paled in what he's become, victim mirroring victim. And so the game begins of wiping it out before it can give voice to what we've had done to us. Victor, I say, but this is not Victor, and he will not pretend anything this time. This time he will not humor.

This time perversion weakens as it latches on. Here is what shame hoards. It wants me to crawl. I have touched others. The heart will go black with the sense of that, for what it has touched in me soils. I must hide this. What I see within the man before me is accidental.

"Let us keep our secrets," I say to which he throws me down, and Nor, who doesn't understand his role in this, Nor, who's inebriated, and befuddled from his fall, observes me in the air as I hit the wall. I lift a hand to my chest and fear panics as I try to call out. *Nor.* But I'm falling and the world spins darkly, closing over my eyes until there is just falling and the brush of skin against my arm.

"We are the same," he says, so that I want to destroy any softness I had.

What is this dark thing and what framed it? When it was my own hands punching the glass, leeching the blood in anodyne, something was released, but it calls forth legions on external grounds, and I know myself no match for it. Until I can harness the stray within, until I can claim what has atrophied and call it to my side, I am no match, for the shadow knows no death in the severance. I have slept so long with this thing, loved its animal, and now my pact with the darkness has drawn in on all sides. I call to it. I call to all that has atrophied, beckon to it, pleading with it to stop while preceding its strike with a fall. Cut me, or I will cut myself. I fear what I ask as I draw you near.

The longer Nor denies the more I will suffer, for one needs the devil's hands, a touch of shiver, something to take them out. How long will this go on, this play with him in the margins dragging along like a drunk? And the dark queen whispering into his ear? Hold on, Nor, she will have you yet, and so it is a shriek that pulls him through, the call of a girl who cannot stop what is happening. Then he is sober and transplanted into falling and the falling has a fluid sound. In it he hears a monotone voice, a stream rushing on without break.

I am on a gray tiled floor trying to remember, trying while fighting my mind to be wrong. But being right fascinates me. I have seen into him. I cannot deny my excitement in reeling in such a fright. How many others know the dark patch in this man? His intentions are wicked, something perverse. Since when have I become so perceptive of shame? We are all capable of the egregious, but this man is loose.

Before me drops the black winged one. Here I will die. The black smudge within the chest presages this and the weight tells me not to fight. A voice curls like a banner wavering on stale air and wrapping me in. I hate who I am. I hate the curiosity that has brought me here all the while knowing that this hatred spawns the man.

"Get up," he says, and strikes, the back of my head slammed into forgetting.

What will it matter when I am nothing like this, that I allow myself to be dismantled so lightly? What is there of self? Where is the warrior? Why stand down? *The crane in obeisance. Feminine divine.* Where is the thing that would rise?

Nor knows before Aurora hits the ground, before the sun glowers from her orange throne, what type of scene this is. He will walk the hills, something following, the cows pacified, the stream darkly meandering, the low fence barely visible in the dark surround until it cuts into his calf. He is crazy with her scent, crazy with the ambivalent search, crazy with the after if he's right. And there is the bird standing before him in the lawn.

How should he have known that the bird had gotten in? How should he have known she'd split her back? That the girl's suffering kept her safe? How could he have been aware of these things and lived? The woman who burns with what she brings to the world and the angel who drags her not aware of her might and the blackbird shattering jars, releasing darkness in a torrent, thrashing beaks against trunks. Again the angel will drag her, this time to the edge, that black facade, that drowning pool, that place of beginning, the nothingness before there was life.

WHAT ENDS THIS.

The crone crosses the floor toward him, eyes held closed with a remnant of black wing. She staggers across the hem of her dress, tearing brocade, as the turret drags. What is there, and where has she come from? Does she live as she falls against his arms, her pallid skin tearing like river birch, the soil of melancholy cursing him with its mood? The old woman slumps to the ground, head rent in her hands, the dark mass of her now dipping into mud, the skin on her face lifting like the pages of a book through which breath is released. A dying book, a fallen tree, the shredded bark, the welted page. Beautiful tragedy.

Behind her in the distance, Aurora's body lies in mire, her face sallow and drawn, her skin the ashy color of her ashy garb. Aurora. A bellow escapes as she arches from the floor. What is this black smudge through the chest where her heart once lay? What is this heaviness in her limbs? If there were some warm thing, but darkness, soot, and that white dress plastered to the ground. *Aurora.* Nor's voice is slow; the words stripped of might and so drowning themselves out, not believing anymore they hold power in this world.

Her lips have purpled like an obstinate winter child, although that spirit in her too has died. A pulse of breath comes sporadically over her bottom lip, and he can only think of a segmented worm, the thought of which sickens him with its baseness. The dampness hardens his bones against the ground and he feels the deep ache of age. You are a fool, he thinks, a cad and a fraud. *Aurora*, he tries again, the name hoarse in his throat so that he chokes a bit then rests his head. The world is dead. He will never muster the strength to move from this place, to stand, or call out. He puts a hand to her throat and holds it there until her eyes shutter open and flash white, close. What watches them seeks pleasure in their demise. It was a sinister thing whose heart, if it had one, elated in their suffering. It smothered itself and took from them its life. Oh, he is tired. He sweeps the hand down across the low gown, fingers the thin silk straps, waits in vain for the life to return his touch. But there is nothing here to return. All that is reciprocated is the melancholy weight of end.

~

Watch the forest wall. In lamplight, in the darkest shades where snow has become the color of a forest floor, where beauty tricks the eyes with subtlety, sky the shade of blank beginning, the blue of the page where night begins deep in winter, the saturated hue where we kneel to take ourselves down. Again. Because what we have imagined fails us. Because Nor is a shade of color incompatible with what we are outside of love. As if we existed here, as if there was not this loss of all that we are in sacrifice. We have still not learned this.

PART 3.

What the hammer? what the chain?
In what furnace was thy brain?
What the anvil? what dread grasp
Dare its deadly terrors clasp?

When the stars threw down their spears,
And watered heaven with their tears,
Did he smile his work to see?
Did he who made the Lamb make thee?

From **The Tyger**,
WILLIAM BLAKE

A FEE FOR THIS PASSAGE.

Something is waiting. There is carrion in the sky seeping out like yellow light, a reminder of what happened to those who did not rise. As always there is a fee for this passage: one must reckon with all she has brought to this place. Here truth embodies the mundane: the trucker rapes flat and plain. So that what surfaces before Aurora is a father in tow behind a man. When I tell you they came at her, the curve of the blade snagging at her top so they could suck at her titties you will know them as men. When I tell you their hands went for her cunt, workman's hands, hands that shook their cocks into the yellowed bowls of the container, that turned the latch on the door and smeared the glass with grime, that they left things in her from under their nails, the little one biting with his little crab mouth you will no longer see the heroine. His leather belt hauled the stench of pine from some drawer. When I tell you he used it to slap his own dick which was flaccid with Zoloft and then strung her by the neck with it, you will wonder what happened to God.

When you get down this far you go alone, and here she is again holding her chest to the black pond seeking something within, the answer at its source. It breathes in her and breathes her in until she sees herself falling and remembers Nor as he fell. The circular band around her neck tightens, and she chokes against the knob in her throat. In the black pond is an opening like fright threatening to erase her. Dark nothing threatens to break out within.

Immerse yourself in it, Aurora, until you find at its reaches a flooded ocean-side town with wet flags of laundry strung through the alleyways, until you find streets unmoored and filling with rainwater on an afternoon exhausted by sun, until you find you can rewrite every miserable moment of your past in this water's depths and still retain the heroine, until you find that this bastard before you has lost hold of the reins. Your hand is at the belt tugging it free and you're climbing the yellow strap toward the man who would have hung you there and raped your dangling body like some abandoned belfry.

Rewrite it all and pack it within or sling it to your back so that when you reach the perimeter and find the sneering face there is no hesitation as you tear into his rubbery cheek.

Blood, rust, I open my eyes and spit a mouthful of flesh. I wipe my lips, swallowing against warm metal and gagging on something soft as a man stumbles toward me from the distance his head held low, shoulders high like the scrapper who kicked my face in. The angel is above me like some sort of raptor awaiting the end but drawing to neither one side nor the other. It is not his fight. (It was never his fight.) The weight of a lurch throws me back toward the abyss, a rock punching into my back, knocking out the wind as I fall and the angel swoops down, blinded by the darkness that swarms. He cannot see what has caused it at these depths, can only sense shadows and struggle, which thicken in him as his heavy limbs sink in flight so that he's more zeppelin than angel. The beginning, he hears in my voice.

Something begins here. I slink like a cat out of the dark, hungry and arrant, and facing the man with a roundhouse kick that slips off his shoulder and spins me to my knees in the mud. Laughing, he shakes his filthy hands on the back of his jeans. There is something in his face that degrades. He is still laughing his filthy laugh, still wiping his hands, still stepping toward me when I wheel around and drag his salacious mouth to the side. Don't wait for recovery, something in me says as my leg rises and a kick plunks into his thick chest and sticks there, trapped. His hands move over it, lecherously groping beneath my pant leg, koi stroking flesh into prickle before he twists, shredding me calf to knee.

Mud and wet muck. A hand in my hair. A stench plugging the senses. Black pain and the crane of a man pivoting and tipping down over me like machine, swinging my head back into his face with the tilt of a lever, tipping his mouth to my lips. Darkness recoils low within and I follow its retreat tripping over my own body, scrambling to my knees. But his temper grows his speed and pain rips again through the back of my head, a whistle leaking out as he careens into my chest and pushes his wiry face into my neck, nuzzles my breasts like a heated dog. I smell his scalp, the rot of crotch, the putrid warmth through his jeans, all he's been made to restrain.

My nostrils are flaring, a knob of blood being sucked in and out of one side. I'll kick his jaw clean of his face. I'm gnashing my teeth and slavering like some animal thing. If I am sore that soreness is black as I stomp the heel of my boot into his throat and blood and dirt spray up from the ground. Then I'm stomping and stomping my boot into his throat before something catches me off-balance and I'm rolling to my back, still kicking, still depressing my heel into the dirt, a truck spinning its tires, my chest a hive of bees. Breath burns. My palms sting. If I don't want to kill him I should stop Nor warns as he swoops down low over the broken man. But this one is never coming back, I swear before falling on him in a tirade.

"Ror," Nor cries. My fists are bloody mallets held aloft and my visage, as I turn my head up, greets him in red savagery from the darkness. "Stop now," he supplicates, causing me to collapse exhausted onto the man's chest, my head falling to the space below his chin. A huff of breath comes splenetic and hard as I bash him again with my fist. In the stillness that follows heat rises into my skin and moisture pools between my breasts, runs down my temples and neck. Blood, rust licked from my cracked lips.

It is not long before a scream passes through clipped closed by the hand on my throat lifting me into the quaking mien of the resurrected son. I rake a handful of dirt from the ground and shove it in his face before throwing a fist to his crotch. I pull at his sack through the gathering canvas, squeeze the rolling knob to a pulp until a cuff to my head releases a warm rush of blood through my nose and I fall in a heap to his side. Over the garbled cussing of the emasculated thing, slumped and coddling his goods, a shadow will fall, and he will lift his head in perfect synchrony with my boot.

How I clench hatred in my teeth, how I tear at his eyes, mangling what slides beneath fingertips, what I will peel like fruit, what I will bash and bash and bruise. Flesh puddles below my fists, how fast it swells, how fists might splash into cheeks, how the sound might make me less afraid, how it might beat as naturally as a heart into the thin skin of the neck, how my hands might bounce elastic off the trachea drum. His hair sticks to my fingers. Everything smells of blood, and I hate and hate and hate what human does as he rises into my enclosing hands. A twist and his torso drops.

Sand. The pit. My hands on the animal, the warm heavy thing in my hands, and then I, too, drop.

I hiccup and choke on a sob, feel the leaky pull of erasure, a paroxysm of glee, hysteria whirling, something arresting the body, drawing out of it a growl that grates the instrument of throat, holds it out long and ragged, before seizing me in a fit of cries as Nor flits about erratically overhead.

RETREAT.

"Where are we?" I ask, having risen numbly from the darkness, Nor following above. The darkness dims in our retreat, and he is astounded to hear the hand still pressed to my throat, the animal slipping in its own blood down the walls of the pit.

"We'll keep moving until we come to something." For he knows there's no way back from this.

I grope at my throat searching for swelling. It could be late dusk for the light in the sky. Strange that it appears not to be coming from the horizon but directly overhead. Finally able to descend, Nor notices the purple blotches coloring my skin so that the feathers that drop from his wings audibly hit the ground. I watch in reflection his horror as through the mud-stiffened hair, I feel the tenderness of wounds. A patch has been torn from my head, and it's matted with blood at the source. I wince in awareness. The rest of me is sprayed with dirt, my top hanging like a rag, breasts free and streaked with mud.

When laughter bounds out of me, it is unconstrained, petals of it alighting like physical things in torpid breeze, my breasts freeing themselves of their casts of dust. It is laughter so hard it preens the lungs and shudders out its pain. It catches Nor who enters it heartily, purring like a heron, and our bodies shake from the magnitude of release, emptying in hysteria that resonates all around. Vacancy.

I slide the straps of my tank top down my wounded arms, and the laughter stops as suddenly as it began. A last note from

Nor dies. I wipe my eyes and shift the tube of fabric over my chest before replacing the straps again. What is left is purified; the body's light a quiet white. It is strange, I think, not needing love, not touching or clinging or needing anything.

We have only our bodies to sense the world and that thing outside of us that knows we are human. What stalks me like a vigilant soul is myself. If I close my eyes, I can feel its judgment through the trees. It is my judgment. It pities and questions and doubts, and moves about me casting fear. The light changes, darkens into a saturated brown. Before me, a lantern appears, shining in its own light, an octagonal form with elaborately carved panels. It hovers before us, spinning slowly on a band of light then dissipating into darkness as we proceed and another forms ahead.

"It's the light realm," I whisper and when Nor eyes my soiled face more feathers molt from his wings. I hear them like slippered steps behind me, like a figure lurking beyond. Fear is rife in me, and my vision darts across the surface of trees attempting to penetrate the darkness. A magpie casts an elastic hymn. Where is the presence of the one beyond? Where have you gone, I question. Wind sweeps the chest clean, vacuous. I stumble and hold on, my left ankle stinging where it catches a branch. I will not make it out of here alive a feeling tells me as I step forward and sink to my ankles in what feels like mud. I'm held fast and sinking deeper, mid-calf, dropping like lead to my knees in the vat. My voice is numb; a paroxysm of despair slipping to my waist, drawing mud over and into the chest, drawing it like water into an empty vessel, filling what had been hollowed in fear. My neck. The stench proliferates as it forces the cry out of and fills my open mouth.

Nor turns in time to see the top of my forehead, my hair following like a cord sucked into a doll. The dim light overhead has not moved. What governs this world is not the same as what governs ours. This could be a room for the lamp's stagnancy. Is it a room? Although he has not spoken the question aloud it resonates in an echo throughout the cavernous depths of this hell. A room. Room. Oom. Oom. He is only now aware of his solitude and the stillness of his own thoughts.

His hand retracts. He fears the mud. In Aurora's absence he fears everything about him, the brown light arcing artificially out of the sky, plaguing him with guilt so heavy he wallows in it until it sinks him to the ground. What sort of angel is he? What sort of coward, cowering at the edge of the mire? And how many times has he failed her now? If he would save her, he must enter the mud. But it is as if stubbornness grew in physical form, locking him within his own reservations. And so he torments himself on its banks, too heavy to feel the presence of the one who's newly arrived.

INTERRED.

I want to go home, I plead with the darkness. Go home. Home. Om. Om. A chorus of voices expands like mockery into the sludge. "Om," I repeat and all of the voices fall away, their vibration creating warmth, rainbow-colored hues of swarming light, though I cannot yet open my eyes. "Om," I whisper again for the companionship of the voices that sing along. In the resonance that follows, I feel the loss of someone close to me and trace the memories to things that feel so far off I cannot mourn. I will not seek Nor in this place. He is memory; our time passed. Something skims my lower belly, my hip. "Aurora," he searches so close to my body I feel the eel-like brush of skin.

BELL JAR.

The same barriers that hold him from the mud block his ears and imprison him. Yes, if one walks a bit to her left she can make out the transparent walls warping the shapes of trees in the background and the ceiling where the light is hung, a bulb tied in brown paper. It will burn, and then he will know.

Don't fight it, Nor. She is meant to go there alone. When you are faced with resistance, be smart and don't fight. There is a reason for it. Try another path.

The solace of this penetrates as the paper catches fire. He smells it at first then feels a gloaming, which shifts his gaze upward as ash drifts down and embers streak his wings in patterns that could have been drawn. He bumps against a wall, startling himself, his movement stunted by something he can't see. His hands pass over the glass cage. He lifts his wings to their height and lets them fall in a gust that if only for a moment extinguishes the flame before it resurges. It is long enough for him to see that the hole that has burned through the ceiling is wide enough for his passage. A stroke beyond the mouth of the cage, fire blazes forth again. He grapples to steady himself midair, his wings, singed and disheveled, failing him then severing open as he turns in the mud on the ground. He feels the girl beneath him.

This game torments him, being aware of her presence and yet absence. What time is it? He cannot read the sky. How long has she been down there? Is there a chance she's not dead?

THE BENEVOLENT FIELD.

And so it was not at the edge of the chaos but here after relinquishing the self completely that I could seek passage. But passage into what? The mud is a temperate body. The colors continue to morph and to bend. What is it before me that protrudes in face? Is it my own I look out of, for there seems to be a hide I gaze out from within? A creature behind another creature. Before me, the sockets deepen my skin. I do not understand.

I am in a sea of animals, the stench of urine strong. It proliferates like black tea steeped in ammonia, stinging my eyes as I open them and try to lift my head above the herd. My ear ticks like a stressed nerve. When impulsively I try to suppress the cadence, I find myself attached to a hoof, lifting it and setting it down, like some puppet thing. The ticking continues, the beasts huddling more tightly together, so that it is impossible for me to arc my head down. I try to shove them back, to make some space around me by swinging the bulk of my haunches—the bulk of my haunches!—to which the animals shift like current before closing in again. A whirring attracts my attention to the right, and I swing my head, once, twice, three times to the side when the pesky thing lands above my eye, which begins to pulse like my ear. It flies off only to land on my left nostril. When I blow out, trumpeting an alarming horn, it scatters the herd. What skittish things, I think, rearing up in fright and then trotting across the blue field after them. I am mesmerized by my knobby legs, covered in thin white fur with shoots of coppery curls.

Tap the ground with a hoof and a sweet scent rises up and an urge to roll the muzzle across the blue cornflowers littering the field. Their delicate petals tickle my face as I tear a patch from the ground and gnaw leisurely at the fruitful bouquet. The grinding sensation, the broad teeth, the lower jaw unhinging and rotating upward, mashing the tender flowers into paste recall joy in me. Lazily, I graze then bask in the warm spring sun, vaguely remembering somewhere I would go. But the sunshine is so warm and the flowers like ether, and the thought doesn't occur to me again.

Days pass like this. A sweet fragrant rain plashes down, a calf joins me, and we romp through the cooling shower, clipping our hooves against the protruding granite rocks in an ode to the rain. We stray beneath a tree where others have wandered and since settled down, chewing their cud while listening to the voice of the rain through the leaves.

In this animal, I will learn how to exist by letting go. So much is instinct, I will find. I will assimilate quickly, remaining a part of this animal world until my soul, fulfilled, longs in other ways to grow. Then in a late summer storm as I doze off in a damp moss bed, I will see the angel's form over mine in the grave. Like this, I will take on his sadness, he leaning over the smooth dark earth of my bed, his feathers falling. I will feel them like wet leaves, magpies, the voice of erasure calling out a name, lowing until lowing grows louder, until it touches me. Had I hands I could gather them. Is this why he's crying? Had I hands and a voice. The lowing grows louder, startling me awake. The cattle are rising and moving away. I can feel the earth tremor as I open my eyes.

The angel is kneeling before me with his pale skin and broad, sad face. His white-green eyes are startling, the nearness of the chiseled torso, naked and erect, the denuded forms jutting out behind, for I have been in the pasture so long that in contrast to my companions, the angel is foreign and slight. It is not that I do not recognize him, but that the smoothness of his face is striking and the brazenness of its features arranged on a flat plate, so that when he sets out a hand to touch me, I scramble out of reach, a protrusion of weathered branches poking into my back.

Understand that to the angel things aren't fixed in form. When Nor descends, he encounters not a herd of cows but complex beings of light, so that every thistle, every strand of web generates a vibration that draws light from its source. Within the herd, Aurora glows. It is not until she speaks that she transforms into flesh, for this is how he has known her. The pasture has restored vigor to her cheeks, and when she scrambles away from him on her hands and her heels before knocking into the base of a tree, he sees a farm girl ruddy with life. The unruly auburn tresses frame a face streaked with mud in which something childlike has returned, a happy lightness he recognizes from what feels a past life.

ON THE UNDERSIDE.

Black earth sticks in the back of my throat and coats my body in mud. I am alone clutching an empty hand, gasping, unused to my lungs. I wrap my arms around my chest and lie for a while, gazing up at the sky where the arced canvas awaits my imagined fate.

"My desire to touch returned my hands," I say, breathing more easily. And so they are still my hands, or those resembling mine. But if I were to examine them, what might I find? We are as we see ourselves.

"I thought I rescued you," Nor returns, shifting his head in the dirt so that he faces me.

"To think, just beyond the surface," I whisper, "had you tried."

Silence.

"I discovered something when I was down there that wants to live," I say, sniffing at the dirt on his skin then rubbing the rich, pungent scent into my cheek. "The field returned me to a place my spirit knew long ago, before doubt and shame and…" I stop myself abruptly. We are lying in a forest of broken trees that jut into the air like walking sticks, trees stripped of their branches, trees with no leaves or stems. Atop the shallowest in the distance sways a bird gutted on the pole. "No, I don't want to define it in terms of not. What it was woke the child and set her inside a field of sunshine with warm lazing animals with strong backs, so that there was nothing but to rollick and revel and renew."

If I were to stay here I might know happiness; I might learn to take a different path; I might learn to create things anew. But on the underside of my convivial mood roams a staid companion, old things grown of the world, what exists in human consciousness in proliferation: limitation and lack, fear and doubt, melancholy and loneliness. We have grown so accustomed to their presence that without there seems deficiency, that sense of absence enough invitation for them to return as if we beckoned them. I take Nor's hand again to my cheek before raising myself to my elbows.

"Show me where the dark thing lives that I might vanquish it," I say in desperation, sensing what lurks beyond. What is it in the taste of the soil that says I no longer belong?

"It is part of the self. We cannot eradicate it. Do not ask anymore what it is or from where it comes, and it will no longer seethe and grow." But I am still asking the same questions, and isn't it too late for all of this?

The perimeter is rife with darkness. If I want to go any-where, I must follow discontent where it leads, for discontent inspires movement and change. We cannot have satiation without first lack, relief without pain and so on. It is only the way of things, dead or otherwise, the questions within us leaking out. Therefore, expecting it to be difficult if not impossible to get out of this depression alive, I nearly topple over an enormous beetle manifest in the path. Another passes underfoot, fear and negativity luring them, when a cool wind draws a shade over the light. In a panic, I stomp my feet. In a flash, the black form ceases to crawl. Nor nudges it with a stick he's plucked from the brush until it animates and scurries aside. Meanwhile, the swarm before us has grown thicker, and hundreds of carapace blacken the ground, their concentric movement propagating the clouds overhead, gathering and pulling the gray masses down, stirring them in storm. There is the smell of dark rain as scattered leaves rise into the vortex, uncovering and doubling the size of the swarm.

A cloudburst disperses the dirt in craters, causing the bee-tles, which fly up in a fervor, to rattle against the trees in a panoply of sound. Nor loses no time. With what is left of his wings arched over us, he pulls me against him and breaks into a low ascent across the sky. He scans the forest floor, his hand on my naked flesh through the fury, his missing feathers hindering flight, a thousand things distracting the angel in this rain that pulls the world into strands. Up ahead the bird sways wildly on its post, perhaps in warning, for the earth at that moment opens into gorge and sucks us down. The cold mud is shuttering the angel's wings, his grip tightening and falling away. Our hold on each other severed, we're swept off in the current of a raging stream, singularly riding the water down, attempting to hold the head above the surface, straining the core, the jolt of rocks poking into buttocks and thighs. My body's jerked, my ankle jarred. Water rushes my mouth and face. I'm flailing my arms to stay buoyant while leveraging against a rock to pry myself free. Something rises out of the water, and I am buoyed into the flow of a river that seems to be widening with the ache in my aching arms.

A skein of geese overhead lets loose a slam of cries. I crank my legs beneath me like I did as a child, spinning and spinning and scanning the sky until my neck burns from strain. I'm alone. The sky is a paler shade of the muddy river. Up ahead I imagine I can feel the solidity of a dock, the warped silky wood breaching the surface, pocked and grooved. I imagine the musty depths of its undercarriage; how algae clings to the edges, around and in between boards until I can actually feel the river pushing me, this great pulsing vein supporting long strides. I dip my arms into its pools and glide, propelled toward a post of the slippery thing until it's the post of a tangible render I'm flinging my legs around.

Arms shaking in strain, I inch upward and curl my fingers over the top edge of the sandy boards. My bottom is an anchor holding me stuck in the river as I try to raise myself by my arms, only noticing then the limp swell of ankle when it buckles on the post. It throbs and I cling to the dock, water bowing around my back. The pads of my feet are fat and numb when something rubbery and elastic sweeps past my legs. In fright, I shimmy hand by hand down the length of the dock, the eel-like thing slithering and carving past, until I'm slipping into loose sands to my thighs, into the legs of stockings two sizes too large, until I'm pulling myself up by a patch of weeds and collapsing onto the matted grasses of the shore. When I roll onto my back, everything aches. Around me the earth extends in burnt-red hue beneath a pallid chartreuse sky. Wearily, I lie there listening to the soughing of creatures in the grass, creatures that writhe like the river, green and black ribbons tipped toward my wrecked form. Rivulets trickling with the turn of the earth. My head is heavy with heat and the stench of drying, which pulls sleep into a form.

Get up, Aurora, you don't know where you are. In this way I fight my body into crawling, my hair a sticky mass that tugs at my arms and scalp. Where is my angel? And what language had covered his molting wings?

I sense a presence skirting along out in the distance, but when I turn my head there is nothing but red earth lain out like… *Like what, Aurora?* Like a fertile plain of beginning. Like God saying yes, it's okay to dream. What dreams would heal the damage that we've done? These are mine. Nor, it's all we've spoken of. It's my own tresses thrown to the ground.

We never start with nothing; the blank page is an illusion. Listen. The stories and the path our dream takes. Oh Aurora, there is no blame. The heaviness the landscape causes within you is only its bareness, and what you think you must conjure from nothing is already formed. It exists within you. What you have to do is only open and let it fly.

So that there before me in the sky above a field shorn of crop is an ancestor scattering grain, a succession of bodies falling from the back of his hand across the stubbled husk, blue fists in a pile, women thrust down, dead dolls slapping each other alive, each flushing the next body white as they plunk down in a shower of dry rain.

Large as a god, my grandfather grimaces, pale hair cropped straight like a boy's, grin slammed askew. He lifts his leg like a dog, grimacing as he shifts his weight onto a twisted arm. Does he see me? An answering kick sends me to the other end of the field like a little gray mouse, his eyes following me down. I begin plucking seeds from the ground in my nervousness, spilling seeds into my mouth in distress. It is cold and the motion warms, the scavenging, the hurry. One by one, I pluck them, collecting them and taking them in handfuls to my mouth. They taste like hiding, dry cases of shame and shameful nubs of shameful meat that come to rest in sharpness in my belly, that cut into me as I bend. The sky is burnt umber, my tank top a rag. My body is a field the wind has dragged through mud, ridges encrusted, I'm swollen with salt. I dig and rebury, rebury and dig when the shadow of a boot comes down from overhead and flattens my hand to the ground. Hand trapped, so small in the darkness, the other creeps out and away over the rich earth. It finds a stray seed and shoves it into my mouth. I do not move my eyes from my grandfather's. So small. Lidless.

Darkness pads the perimeter.

His hands fall like bars to my shoulders and he throttles the broken coffer of my body until it comes loose. The corset springs away, thread unraveling into his arms, all that I am spilling out in shreds into his hands, into knotted tools, into barbarous prongs and touching him inside where if he remains long enough, hands embedded in his own flesh, beyond denial, beyond pain, he'll touch something else.

Then he is gone, the coward, and the dark shade at the back of the field again recedes. It is dusk as I loop the corset strings around the pegs and cinch it tight. The paper lifts and scatters and I scavenge for more seeds in the dying light, swallowing and swallowing until the fibrous things swell in my belly and I find myself sickening, my hand pressing something flesh, a shoulder, a knot, and from it the bloom which will cripple my grandmother's back.

I fold myself into her side and watch the last of the persimmon sky, wet petals of lotus flowers dying and drawing in. For there is spectacle in all that surrounds us, and the loneliness that has beckoned the man behind the trees has dissipated into majesty. Along the river's far bank comes a white gloaming, an orb in gust swaying on a pole, a child's lantern.

"The more who listen and follow their paths the stronger the creative force grows in us. In other words, the closer the gods come, the louder they grow." There is a figure across the river, a body obscured in ambient light. "All is driven by self. Have you understood this yet?"

Then the form is gone though its radiance remains. In it, I will sit and wonder when such knowledge is of use, I with my terrible decisions. Maybe in the past I wanted to know darkness, maybe I was successful in this, in my exploration of the depths. Maybe there were two selves and the one with sinister dreams won out. How marvelously I mastered depression and despair, the destitute wanderings of a shade through the margins of a dream. Maybe I was the queen of lurid things; maybe what had struck me and wrung me out was part of what I am. I wonder if it doesn't strengthen me that I need not hide from it now. But am I so in love with suffering that I would imprison myself forever when what I want is the antithesis of all I've known? Beneficent black charmer, you sorcerer and seductress, today we will align.

Sulfur pools open out in the distance, tufts of green in an expanse of white sand. The sky is blank blue, startling blue and all is so still that one hears the arid surround like a bird piped clean, or the remains of a sea once pulled through the sky.

We are beautiful to ourselves and then to the world, in the words of Margaret Choo. It is the same with ideas, I think, as I fashion out of river birch a pair of rustic wings which will arc from my back as if framing some new thing. We tell the world of our discoveries. We hail them as great and release them into the world as gifts that allow the world to grow. Here, I say, reaching out my arms: a curious pioneer of bright things. Polished light laughs out of me...

OUT OF DARKNESS.

…and then drops into the sand where it hisses and goes out. When I look around again everything is black. Why is darkness so familiar, so safe? I rise like a child into a dream world. Eyes closed or opened, it makes no difference, internal and external are one. And that is what this place does, collapses the façade so that what is revealed is true form. For a while there are only my thoughts coloring things until a voice speaks. Before me the beard of an old male god, the god's breath rising in dark garnet orbs that drift out and away. What is this place? I think of the cows in the beneficent field and see them before me.

The god chortles, and his face appears in pink and salmon streaked light. "Show me a swan," he says, and before his lips close on the word a wing eclipses him, the long orange beak rimmed in black, the open black nostrils, onyx wings stretching out and slapping the river, endowing it with mystery as light beings surface and dive. Flight inhales the path over the water. Ham-sa. On the exhale, it will return to the earth. "Hatred." Symbols scored in a woman's flesh; wings marred with calligraphy. The scent of burning. "Love."

"What?"

"Love." My mouth opens. A hand.

"Out of nothing you created the world as you've experienced it." I see his face again, the rest of his body conjured more slowly, the ruddy complexion, the swollen hands. "As you've demonstrated, this is our first dilemma, how to free the creator from what has come before. Associations only bring the same." He stops as if he doesn't quite know where to begin, how to tell this story to the body, how to take me beyond where I've been. "It is as you'd imagined with the weather report when you allowed yourself to perceive an invented future world," he continues. My confounded expression prompts him to add, "In the book, Aurora. In the book." In open-mouthed wonder, I listen as he recites for me the page I've destroyed.

The meteorologist, as a doctor of astrology and physics, would recognize weather as a precipitous outburst of temperament somehow responsive to the human condition. By enigmatically preserving the mystery of the future event, hinting of its wondrous resonance within us and from us, hinting of the connection between human and surround, the meteorologist would give an inspired reading of our shared atmosphere. In other words, the weather would be an extension of human. I remember now how I'd imagined it, how at one time I'd thought I spawned the clouds. How glorious the concept was then in the next instant damned. For wouldn't the men break it? Wouldn't they try with their exploitative notions and hands crushing everything?

When the north wind breaks through the region, something of your self will break off and drift. On hearing this, the men would close down, clamp tight the hatches and fight with all their will against its truth, and so it would not come to pass and they would be right. *But another storm will form off in the distance and it will be their storm and we will call it "Denial" after them and it will be fierce and its fog will not lift for days.*

I clap my hands in remembrance. Oh, how within me he lives!

"And so you have illustrated the second obstacle in our path: expectation." He's beginning to take on aspects of Dr. Rutch. "How can we create a new world when parallel to our creation we are tearing it down with responses based on perceptions from the present day?" He lets a silence pass in the form of a long gap in the wind. "Not long ago people told themselves stories riddled with heroes and gods. The gods had their hands in the affairs of humans and the humans supplicated the gods. There were some who were godlike in the favor bestowed on them. You are one of them, Aurora."

(Here is the one within who bolsters us with fancy, who allows us to dream.) I nod in comprehension, and the god continues.

"What we are is essentially what we become when we let ourselves be what we were created to be. It just so happens we are emphatically and ecstatically in love with this person. All of her ideas and proclivities are perfect for us."

"The divine self," I answer.

"Yes, the self in everything. Within you the creator guides. Align with her. This is where you live." My thoughts drift to the crone. "Your desires are her desires. She lives through you, experiences life through you." But no, the crone wasn't God, but maybe an aspect of God… "Work with what has come before," he continues, breaking me out of my thoughts, this figure filled with bounding light, beneficent. "In this way we discover what we want in terms of realizing what we don't want. The images being written of the bleak future, for instance, toward which we find ourselves unwittingly catapult-ed: barren landscapes and war, the suffering and violence and lack depicted in literature and films. As much as one might claim they are stories, they are filling the human consciousness with visions, and it is toward these visions that we progress. Apocalypse. Desolation. It is only for lack of imagination that it continues. Therefore, new stories need to be written." He pauses, making sure I'm getting this. "For us to envision the future in a new light."

"I am to write the future."

"Yes, you've known this for some time, and now you know where to begin."

'I must create a system or become enslaved by another man's,' I remember.

"Passively, another man's world prevails, the stories he tells instances of our failure, for it is his future that we are moving toward, gradually his steel world, his apocalypse, earth the color of dead imagination, the color of soil meant to bear the same crop. Why? Why remain here, stagnant at the hands of all that has failed us?"

Ah, that's why the crop, my grandfather. The cycle of violence perpetuated.

"It is in questioning that we receive answers; in imagining that our futures are born. How many limitations we construct on our own. Our creator is within us and we within the creator. What we draw what we write what we visualize culls us from the depths and uses us as instrument. Perhaps this is the greatest challenge, for in it the vastness of the blank page. Endless possibilities. Begin again. Move on in thought to advance the world. Write us out of the desert. Write the natural world back in."

Stillness. I close my eyes, or perhaps they were already closed. It does not matter; inner and outer are one.

THE CHOSEN ONE.

"Wisdom is indivisible from the spiritual realm."

"So I am chosen?"

"Aurora, we are all chosen. You want to know if your role is of greater importance because you're given insight into the nature of God? You see things because you have the desire to see them and the ability to interpret the signs. Your eyes are cast toward something other, and so it recognizes you and responds. Those who are complacent with the material world see only that. How many people do you know who've had some sort of spiritual encounter, yet who accept it as an exception, divine intervention evidencing God but of no greater importance than that? People whose dead loved ones have stepped in and protected them from harm, or others visited by angels? Their lives go on as planned, the event merely coinciding with a Christian ideal."

I am lethargic, brought down by the suggestion that I'm somehow not The One.

"The things you house within, what you are drawn to, what you see yourself accomplishing when you allow yourself to dream, these are divine. The ones who go on to attain these things are the chosen ones, for it is within the warrior's soul that we are capable of greatness. You know what you are. Do not let the world tell you it's a disorder. That you can fly from one extreme to another demonstrates your humanness and grows your compassion for the world and your capacity to know it, and so your strength. That you have sat within dark moods in an attempt to glean wisdom, to ascertain a source which you might then render in words. Do not fear what you will become. It has happened already.

"When you realize this, it scares you and you dwell on what you lack. But what you know from empirical study, what you know of mental illness as it manifests within the creative mind, this is your area of expertise. Do not degrade it."

"So where do I go from here?"

"Sometimes our powers only manifest in need."

WICKEDNESS.

"It isn't hard to find evil in this world," said the witch. "Evil is always more easily imagined than good, somehow."

From **Wicked**,
GREGORY MAGUIRE

"Nor," I whisper. Something is poking into my back. When I open my eyes, I am on a strand, and Nor is there touching a protruding branch. Wings, I think and imagine I feel them, for here I can be anything. Why then the ship? Why suffering?

His eyes open. "You reach again and again for the dark thing. What are you seeking?" He must be a part of what I claim.

"Beauty." The answer comes before I have time to think or process the question.

"There is beauty in other things," Nor says, swallowing against his parched throat.

"But the images that pass feed me tragically."

"It is where you set your eyes."

"No, Nor, it's not. I only open them and look out and there at the window: the orange tomcat trailing its infected scrotum through the toothed weeds, orange red blood as it falls to its haunches and helplessly dips its face below the raised leg, flips again to its feet in pain or fright. Why when I look out the window are these the things I see? Why not butterflies and blossoming trees? Why do I collect these things? What do they wake in me?"

Nor is silent. "It was not beauty," he says somberly.

I know this. There is hollowness in the light that breaks out around us and that brightness enters what within could have only been empty.

"I didn't ask you to see that boy," he says, the theater his surround. But when I turn, it is toward the water, for we are on the beach, the sand chill on my barefoot feet. "Why are you shutting your eyes to this? Why won't you admit what you see? That you, who hail yourself as angel, are the greatest atrocity! Just stop it! Stop drawing them up. Stop luring dark things into the world." His grip is strong. "What do you want my sweet angel?" he says, tapping my branch wings. "You want to be godlike, mighty, and pure? You want an ideal you can't kill? An ideal that you think impossibly trite, but still you want it to be? Goodness, cloying goodness. Why an angel? I ask you. Why me?"

Judgment, deliverance, harbinger of abject things. What does he want me to see? "You shaved your head," I attempt. "For discipline you were like me."

"Yes, Aurora. Cutting away the unruly. Punishing and re-moving what couldn't be tamed. But the dichotomy, my sweet. Admit that you are dark, Love. Admit you like cruel things. Admit that it was your own hands tipping his fingers into your mouth, that the scars you bear draw your amusement. Admit you are human once and for all, that you are cracked, savage, and sane, that malevolence matures you. Admit that you love the fright in me, the command of punishment, the way it silences everything, the way everything stops."

Something in me cracks a smile; there again the deviant laugh. Within the flagellant scours herself. The pleasure of punishment drags in shame; I see its face before me. It is human. It is a man's face, sick in the arc of the knife reflecting the flesh he mars. If you were to see the cutting you'd be sick with it; but know an animal that doesn't want to be paired with other animals, the ropes of wire that bind the flesh circle, that pull one against the other. "I am not like this."

"Maybe God loves being tipped into the lower range." He is not done. "What is human without the capacity to roam? Roam. Leap. But take back the core. Rule with all the things you carry. Leave out not one for fear the repressed show up in your life like a haggard thing you've flayed and tossed off. Let us rule this sweet reckless mess of a self, but let us do it vigilantly."

"I pray at night for the killing to begin that we may begin again in chaos…" A line from one of my poems.

"Yes, Aurora. It was a dark wish from the heart."

It was a wish born of repression, a reaction to denying the self. Is this where it begins? Where the seeds tendril and spawn? Where we swallow that they become part of us because we choose them? That we are the victor as well as his pawn.

The angel, gilded bronze, rises from a saturated sky, drying before the dawn. "It is not the impulse to bludgeon someone to save him from emotional suffering, but the suppression of this very human impulse that breeds shame, and shame that in turn breeds self-loathing and that in turn breeds a desire to escape and so deviation and dis-ease in the mind. Let yourself be wicked at times if only in thought. Don't judge it, for it is the same magnificence that spawns the storm."

The flagellant gives way to the perversion of touch, the man touching him, holding the wings, widening the little boy. Nor curls into a ball. His magnificence dimming in the radiant surround until he is compressed in a metal cage, light leaking out around, his magnificence dimming in his humanness.

"Nor," the man whispers into my ear. And, Nor, no. I see him bent at the angel's side, hear the voice purring into my ear as through a shell. "I don't blame you," he says. He is a man. He wants to touch me.

I lean down, crouching in light that glimmers like glass. "Nor." My lips are swollen. Find the cage and put him back in. The man with his skinny dick hanging out, and how he touches himself and his lips open and he says 'O' and he has a pale gray suit and inside it is so empty that it aches with cold and the light can no longer shine inside. It is gone, the light, and we are a hole, a ditch dug out of the walls. And there is no angel. And we are numb and we scrunch down and we I'm saying we and we will bury ourselves. And we will bury all of the things that have gotten us to this place so that there's only this.

"Keep digging." Nor says. My eyes are closed. Why is it so difficult to love myself I wonder, and he wonders the same thing and we dig and we dig and he is so frail and so pink and so like the member and the space within widens and the emptiness expands and there is nothing here but more sand.

"There's nothing here, Nor, but more sand." I can't hold him without clinging without pushing him within, without balling his wings in my fists. He shakes himself out. There is nothing inside. Then that nothing is opening me. I take his hand inside the thoracic cavity. Metal blood in the corner of my mouth, I feel it open my eyes.

"The only way I won't hurt you is if you won't hurt yourself."

But I don't want to exist anymore.

My gaze shifts. There is only an apparition glinting like sunlight hitting fish in the depths. "The trespass of soul. The more you hollow out of your chest, the greater its power to latch on." Yet there is only cold expansion, a portal emptying me in waves. How can he know any more than I do? I stagger, trying to catch the heart.

There is a place within where it cripples me to go. Metal-cold it expands until breath cannot be captured or ascertained, until there is flight in dying, until nothing claims but a wound of violent consciousness, a cry that never ends. Here darkness is grave and vacuous. Black water leaps at sand. What would be the inversion of wind erodes the landscape, replacing me with what cannot stand. "This is knowledge imparted by gods requiring sacrifice."

We will know things we never wanted to know in this place.

"What is this that…"

"You are opening." The breastplate tears now, the trespass

quickening. "Choose something else," he says.

But I can't and I won't, each intake of breath threatening to go on. *Help. Close me.* I'm traveling away with the sky, the darkness ever elusive with me conjoined and proud. To turn around would mean returning with nothing but an experience rife with pain, a destitute plight, a depleted dream. The darkness would have been deception. Knowing itself to be nothing more, it would have beckoned me. My desire for its wisdom would have grown its might, the more I sought it, the more it having sought existence as if I were defining it, creating it, using its powers as my own, so that I fear now that this is all I am, and that there is only this to know: that I've wasted my life, that I have been a fool, that there is a realm within where it destroys us to go, that it has drawn me, that it has destroyed me, that I am nothing more. What when all I've discovered is the absence of something, a vacuous depth, an open well?

It pulls at me now, cloth being dragged from the opening, like the thorax of a doll that's been stuffed with rags and emptied, the knife purged from the hole. There is nothing here and yet that nothing lives, and yet that nothing strains on my chest and fills me vacuous. Here I am slipping into my core and expanding. Something exists here that has the power to extinguish and I am being extinguished traveling into it, erased through the center of my own being. But it is not erasure. What is this that threatens to replace me? And what am I for standing at its rim?

One of the children teeters out, and Nor raises a hand to stop me before he understands what calls to me: all of them residing, collective pain. Just as the light sought me in darkness, here is the darkness seeking my light. The trip down into body yielding a realm of existence where body opens on a place which bores through all. Here, lungs are torn. They cannot carry you, flesh. Here, we are human in the absence of body. Here, we are God. What you feel is vacuous. If soul expands in the presence of darkness this is soul, if soul were what sought container, what poured into a vessel took that vessel's form, no matter what form, no matter if infinite. It is how I know I am more than a body, for I maintain a consciousness even when plunged to its depths. It is how I know I belong to a source that has its source in all. What draws me here in my quest, what says I'm the one to discover these things cannot be wrong... *what wishes to reveal itself must also reveal its antithesis.* And so in darkness, light, extinguishing, birth: a place of dying where we begin again. We belong to these things; we have our hands in all.

God has taken its vessel in life. And then it is clear to me. Dark things exist because we want them to. Our intrigue creates them, our desire to know, from where does this come and how cruel can we be and in turn how much cruelty can we bear. We ask our madmen to the stage. Then we lead them around on strings and ask them to show us how.

We are their creators. What we watch, what we read, where we turn our eyes we are choosing. We have chosen all we have brought into this world, and when we decide to put an end to suffering, it will be a collective end. And when we decide we don't want to be victims, when we decide we no longer kill, when we decide we no longer need discontentment and rage, we will put an end to those too. For now, we are human, and so things must destroy and worlds must fall, for the universe is a wondrous child with a vast imagination and simultaneously a wise crone seeking to heal. These things are not antithetical but rather parts of a whole. All regenerates and begins again. What enters the consciousness of the world becomes the world's.

NOT DARKNESS.

I am trying not to ask about darkness, trying not to ask about punishment and rage. I have bred these things in the body. Now I will breed other things.

And so I begin in a northern land in the dead of winter, a land knowing darkness in a year incorrigibly temperate and gray, season following season as if from within a jar packed with sod, watered and shook, in which what grows is shaken again, interred and stunted, the sky slightly paler than the saturated ground. It is midday beneath the murky waterline, and it is sleeting. I can almost pretend it snow that slops heavily down, can almost smell winter's wet woolen clasp in the din of rain on the apartment's glass sky and the white perforations, the white ellipses ticking down faster than thought can complete itself.

Tomorrow I will show you why it is that I am here. Tomorrow that I push further and further away in fear and your mistrust. Wait, I say. And then I will remember, and I will begin again not in reaction, but intention, for this is what I mean to show you... First, taste.

What is that? What are you dusting across the earth? The angel wants to know.

Starch to dry the rain.

I shake the jar and we are dry and silky. Shhh.

What is that?

Creation. A powdery snow softens the appearance of the city until we can get out and be free.

It doesn't bother me to stay. Everything is here that you could want.

That *you* could want. You forget me. The homogenized weather. I can't exist like this. It is flushing me out in distraction, pushing me into the same.

And so the angel rides the train of my dress, the papery white of winter snow. We are the first to mark it, he in tow, as we move out of the city onto a hill overlooking the sea.

"Tell me again what it was to hear the dogs cry into tin, rain fall against the chain-link fence." It is the voice of the wise woman, crone.

"I am trying not to ask about darkness."

"But you know how to strike beauty so that friction warms. Sidle up beside him, against his twitching back."

"Why do you want this to break me?"

"Because it is still raw in you; you haven't finished yet."

"If I live in those memories, I only bring more of the same. Leave it. It's done."

"But if you were to release it."

"Please, leave it. It's dismal enough here without that. Don't you see that is why the snow? It covers and makes things beautiful."

"You confined her in winter. It's part of the tale."

"I heard the dogs and forced them to sleep, so that I could sleep. Is that where I should begin? I forgive myself."

"But these are things that help others live."

"Shall I tell you how it was then to walk the reservoir in shadow? Shall I tell you how it is that my mind functions more slowly now for having been there? How I am not the same?"

"Only because you cannot help it. Now show me for god's sake so that I don't have to go through this again."

When we were children, Obadiah came. Obadiah was a blizzard with drifts so high they came up over our swing set, banked it like mountain ranges, so that as we pushed through a wall of snow came down over us in avalanche, brilliant chips of snow glinting over us snow princesses. Three beautiful daughters. Every one in four will be raped. But we were only three.

We built igloos. I will remember this years later, the sun drawing amber over the panes, how solitude might resonate more deeply in such a memory, my sister's laughter, her oval face and thick, plaited hair, a girl and her peanut-butter-colored dog traipsing across the lawn toward the little one bundled in her pale blue snowsuit hair ablaze in the setting sun. How the light came warm through the wet dark trees and cast itself persimmon on the ground. How in the absence of all these things barn board might gray, old paint haphazardly rolled might reflect the marred, sand and debris scuffed into every step, ground into the knees and palms and skinning the hip when one fell in her panties from the height of the unrailed staircase. Waking later to vomit, then washing cold in my skin the warm oatmeal-pink spray from cheek and hair. Casting the lace-trimmed top into the green hamper, switching off the light while my hand brushed the pink inset of the open wall. Always my hands on the stairs as I climbed. Trying not to wake him. My breath reeking and my skin damply fevered as I curled into myself on the sheets, arms between my thighs.

I clawed at my lips one day, wanting to punish her for keeping us there in this house on the edge of winter.

"Punish who, Aurora?"

Myself. Her. But I'd cut myself before I'd met him. Flung my body down a staircase, sipped codeine pills with liquor so as to silence the berating one within. What causes this, I wondered, slipping easily into the inherited role. (For what we ask for, life will show us. I know this now.) And somehow when the body became too heavy to lift from the sheets, I thought myself eccentric. Suffering had chosen me as it had chosen no other. Here was blackness so foreign that it could only be some divine conjuring; something had picked me out. The martyr in me shrieked for joy, and the will to protect myself gave out on the floor of the bedroom on the plush, gray rug, where I would learn what it was to have a boy move through me into his own pleasure, to push parts of me out of the way while holding onto the breasts of a body quietly perspiring and a voice within saying I don't love you to myself. It was done in punishment, and if it happened again, I'd prefer to be drunk and shut the pretty one off in a room somewhere down the hall or in the basement and let sex with her beautiful curves, sex in a pair of white cotton panties littered with cornflowers, be done.

These memories stir what within would harm her again.

"This is human," the crone responds. "It cannot be any other way. You cannot skip parts."

Like this, something within rattled. I drank myself into bed, confining something else.

"So is the story of human evolving, an organism bringing itself into awareness."

If I have been chosen, then what chose me?

"You have chosen yourself."

The meteor shower, and the light being who finally crept past the stairs to hang herself in front of the dresser. The rescuers worn thin. One knew it would be like this.

"There are only the answers we seek."

I sought darkness. Once I felt it within, I wanted to know it. What power it had that all of what I had been could turn dull; that life could be tedious; that I might not choose to rise one day; that I might will death to come at night as a prayer; that pain could be such that it could masticate a spirit.

I would die here slowly. When it finally came time to leave, there could only be crawling and a self so divided we could no longer fend for her. For whom? What center did she have, she that let herself be treated so? All that she was scrawled on a page in darkness that proliferated with her gaze, what we seek seeking us. I would die here and drag the body off to the edge of a marsh where we would then descend further, body all dark now, cage of wren, flight smudged against a panel of sky, a jar...

I would know then how many I housed, how many children

exist in the self, and how inexhaustible is spirit, how resilient flight, for one might escape as light from a candle, a being seen aspiring, ever in ascent, and that image might live in us. Although returned dark, we would have felt something in the glimmer, would have felt something in the dying out that we had forgotten being dead.

Something would claim us at the base of page that had not been before, and we would slip beneath it, reaching in the body a terrain of absent song, a disassembled lyric, a strained line pushed into an open chest until it stung with music. There would be nothing else then; just this and a strand that in blue skylight took us apart.

I wanted to know this desolation. Why else would I have come? Why else would I have pushed the sky back? Why else would the observer have hung there, exposed, if I had not asked to do it on my own, so that I might see what I had perhaps forgotten? We choose these things. I chose to be a victim. I chose to be raped. I chose to be depressed. I chose to feel what it was like to have someone slip his hands in and control. I chose to be out of control. I chose nothing. I chose to be afraid.

ABRAXAS.

The bird fights its way out of the egg. The egg is the world.
Whoever wants to be born must destroy a world.

From **Demian**,
HERMANN HESSE

And so I reach in and find a place in me destroyed.

  She will have lain so still for so long without hopping,
without jerking excitedly about, without impulsively springing
from the bed, without vivacious gesture, thinking the world
restrained, thinking restraint rewarded, believing what she had
been told about goodness and right: to be good was sexless; a
woman was pure. Then a man touched her head with his
puppeted hand and a child became filth and shame...

AWARE.

You've trawled the depths you've been inside. You know this is how it is. How there is a multiplicity of self when you return. Go down and make it a house with a cellar when the angel descends at the end.

But he does not know why he's down there.

"He brings up the bird, do you see? In descending we rise. In descending a mouth becomes yours. The woman in the throat that you spoke of."

Christ, is this how we finish it?

He clings to me. Nor?

What have I done?

His body is mine. When I touch it is me that I'm touching and I could push him back inside and I would but for the dark wall behind the mask, the gasp in my throat when I saw it. When metal turns, and the burnished imperfections come to the surface, all this dark wood towering about in the cathedral, the dark vacant breath within its nave, what lives and dies without words but mine to say why it was there and what it meant. *In the narthex of the chapel it is night and I breed you, not these voices obsequious to the Father...* But I made it speak with the voice of a god I'd once known, or rather than God, the voice of a prophet or beatific nun. Holy aura shining. A black or white thing we all have known, but this angel in the temple was not one. If Jesus were there at the head of the nave what could this have been but his reflection, his shadow side? But we are more than these things, one and its antithesis, a multiplicity of unexplored arrangement.

What daemon this that *klettert* the walls? What daemon this that freezes? Bare plate feet on a metal snake and a ball. This thing breathed in me when I gasped with the breath of a gun through the glass door of the mausoleum. And I knew when I looked at his eyes that I was looking at something of self and that this self was mirroring something within. Vacancy. No mercy. Here was the absolute totalitarian one, the one that ruled with iron fist, the one that said "Stand down!" Yet how could love also be this thing? For what it stirred was life in me that I could be this thing of maleficence. Maybe I knew then that it was about to get darker as I stood in awe of expanse. Maybe I knew then why the sword and why the shield. But had I known the hand I'd held would be the one that turned my face that day when it hit the wooden stair and became prey.

And if this were, then what of the light? Darkness, too, would be light in negation and so light, and so the light I had been seeing would have been me. Myself outside of myself. Not hallucination, nothing foreign. Sparks coming off the night, flint burning out in the darkness, those glass cages of birds, and the friction of the wings divining spark. Still, who sent them and what were they?

"It's the rest of your self, what cannot be in existence all at once, but what is in existence all at once when one asks to see. You sent them to yourself. Do you get it now? We cannot function all-knowing. We can only say 'I am aware'."

How a god could not possibly be God without knowing it was all... Sparks coming off what was struck, what was formed, what was blown. Something reaching out with its message from a realm of light. That it was a spirit dying, that it was flame ascending a dying form, that it was God touching God with all it could conjure of what a human form might see. Yes, to save me. Yes, to say yes to the walls, to say hold on we are not done yet exploring; hold onto your human form that they caged within might hold on, and I might be at the helm, the destitute one, the failure, the naive girl-child, the maculate virgin, the whore, what threw herself into experience's bed and said take me away from my head, ease the darkness that comes from a girl at war, at war with what is expected, at war with the convention burnt into her skin, a girl learning girl was nothing to live for, that nothing could preface what she'd become, a girl having to crash herself, toss herself to the pavement, bend and be done, a girl saddled and ridden, a girl eaten and bled, a girl of the world and the dead, one saying, I've been one. Oh, I've known you girl.

And I know another one within whom I will become, but will she have fire in her loins, will she bleed?

ACKNOWLEDGMENTS.

Excerpts were published in Garbanzo Volume 3 in a piece titled "Chapters from an Unpublished Novel: A Study in Punishment/Love."

Thanks to my parents for instilling in me the obstinacy and tenaciousness that let me see this to fruition. (The happy book, if I ever write one, is all yours.)

Thanks to my sisters for reading this in its early versions and offering no help whatsoever in saying *it's beautiful* (i.e., letting me struggle a few more years, forced to rely on whatever it is within us that knows this thing already in completion and so leads on).

Thanks to my husband for his patience, trust, and encouragement in supporting the dreams of an aspiring artist.

Thanks to Shanna and Scott for their keen eyes and editorial suggestions.

Thanks to Chryssalis and faestock and the rest of the DeviantARTists behind my cover image. Check them out at www.chryssalis.deviantart.com/art/DOMESTIC-STRANGER-edit-434076596

Lastly, thanks to Marc Moorash, my perfect reader, for the final edit (all errors mine); for the beauty and courage to see beyond under into and between; for recognizing my vision and the way it was shining and simply touching a coattail to its surface and saying there. now.

NOTES.

In an NPR interview with Alisa Weilerstein ("Alisa Weilerstein Plays Elgar: Exploring Music With An Intense Past," December 4, 2012), the cellist speaks of music having a past that deepens with each movement, with each return to the theme, a concept which she attributes to conductor Daniel Barenboim. As Aurora wakes to consciousness and the angel appears, there is a sense of his return—he has been here—and yet he is here for the first time. The story is informed by a past of such weight and intensity that we cannot help but know it implicitly. In the last line of VEHICLE OF A GOD, I make reference to this idea.

"If someone would just blow on my heart," is adapted from a line in Pablo Neruda's "Bacarole" as translated by Donald D. Walsh in *Residence on Earth*.

The reality of a feeling is a concept that comes from Virginia Woolf.

ABOUT THE AUTHOR.

Having spent the past five years as an ESL instructor in Germany, Alana Eisenbarth now lives in the state of Virginia with her husband and cat. She received her MFA in Poetry Writing from Washington University in Saint Louis and her BFA in Creative Writing from the University of Maine at Farmington. This is her first novel.

Visit her at alanaeisenbarth.com for her latest appearances and musings.

Made in United States
North Haven, CT
27 June 2023

38286981R00148